"You are playing u

Hannah gave a wry smil

"Not the kind you will get from me. You'll have to find another man to do the job. I'm not for hire."

She tilted her head to the side. "Do I scare you?"

"On the contrary. It is you who should be afraid of me."

"But I'm not scared of you. I don't care about your reputation. After everything you've done for me, how can I not trust you?"

Francesco shook his head.

"You think I'm worthy of your trust?" Unthinkingly, he reached out a hand and captured a lock of her hair.

Reclosing the gap between them, she tilted her head back a little and placed a hand on his cheek.

"I want one night where I can throw caution to the wind. I want to know what it's like to be made love to, and I want it to be you, because you're the only man I've met who makes me feel alive without even touching me."

Francesco could hardly breathe. His fingers still held the lock of her hair. The desire that had been swirling in his blood since he'd nuzzled into her neck thickened.

When had he ever felt as if he could explode from arousal?

This was madness.

The Irresistible Sicilians

Dark-hearted men with devastating appeal!

These powerful Sicilian men are bound by years of family legacies and dark secrets.

But now the power rests with them.

No *man* would dare challenge these hot-blooded Sicilians...

but their women are another matter!

Have these world-renowned Sicilian's met their match?

Read Luca Mastrangelo's story in:

What a Sicilian Husband Wants

March 2014

Read Pepe Mastrangelo's story in:

The Sicilian's Unexpected Duty

April 2014

Read Francesco Calvetti's story in:

Taming the Notorious Sicilian

August 2014

Michelle Smart

—

Taming the Notorious Sicilian

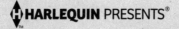

Recycling programs
for this product may
not exist in your area.

ISBN-13: 978-0-373-13269-0

TAMING THE NOTORIOUS SICILIAN

First North American Publication 2014

Copyright © 2014 by Michelle Smart

Printed in U.S.A.

All about the author...
Michelle Smart

MICHELLE SMART'S love affair with books began as a baby when she would cuddle them in her cot. This love for all things wordy has never left her. A voracious reader of all genres, her love of romance was cemented at the age of twelve when she came across her first Harlequin® book. That book sparked a seed and, although she didn't have the words to explain it then, she had discovered something special—that a book had the capacity to make her heart beat as if falling in love.

When not reading or pretending to do the housework, Michelle loves nothing more than creating worlds of her own featuring handsome brooding heroes and the sparkly, feisty women who can melt their frozen hearts. She hopes her books can make her readers' hearts beat a little faster, too.

Michelle Smart lives in Northamptonshire with her own hero and their two young sons.

Other titles by Michelle Smart available in ebook:

THE SICILIAN'S UNEXPECTED DUTY
  (The Irresistible Sicilians)
WHAT A SICILIAN HUSBAND WANTS
  (The Irresistible Sicilians)
THE RINGS THAT BIND

This book is dedicated to all the staff and volunteers at the John Radcliffe Children's Hospital, with especial thanks to the team on Kamran's Ward. Without their care, compassion and sheer dedication, my beautiful nephew Luke would not be here.

This book is also dedicated to the memory of Henry, Lily and Callum.
May you all be playing together with the angels.

CHAPTER ONE

FRANCESCO CALVETTI BROUGHT his MV Agusta F4 CC to a stop and placed his left foot on the road as he was foiled by yet another set of red lights. Barely 7:00 a.m. and the roads were already filling up.

What he wouldn't give to be riding with nothing but the open road before him and green fields surrounding him.

He thought of Sicily with longing. His island had none of the grey dreariness he was fast associating with London. This was supposed to be *spring*? He'd enjoyed better winters in his homeland.

He yawned widely, raising his hand to his visor out of pure habit. After all, no one could see his face with his helmet on.

He should have gotten Mario to bring him home after such a long night, but being driven by anyone irritated him, especially in a car. Francesco was a man for whom *drive* had multiple definitions.

The light changed to green. Before twisting on the throttle and accelerating smoothly, he swiped away the moisture clinging to his visor.

What a country. At the moment it was like driving through a saturated cloud.

As he approached yet another set of lights, a cyclist on a pushbike just ahead caught his attention—or, rather, the fluorescent yellow helmet she wore caught it. She reached the lights at the moment they turned amber. If that had been him, Francesco mused, he would have gone for it. She'd had plenty of time.

But no, this was clearly a law-abiding woman with a healthy dose of self-preservation. She stopped right at the line. The car in front of Francesco, a large four-wheel drive, drew level on her right side.

She had the thickest hair he'd ever seen—a shaggy mass of varying shades of blonde reaching halfway down her back.

The light turned green and off she set, sticking her left arm out and turning down the street in that direction. The car that had been beside her also turned left, forced to hang a little behind her, with Francesco joining the convoy.

The road ahead was clear. The cyclist picked up speed....

It happened so quickly that for a moment Francesco was convinced he had imagined it.

Without any indication, the four-wheel drive in front of him pulled out to overtake the cyclist, accelerating quickly, but with the spatial awareness of a cauliflower, because it clipped the cyclist's wheel, causing her to flip forward off the saddle and land head-first on the kerb.

Francesco brought his bike to an immediate stop and jumped off, clicking the stand down through muscle memory rather than conscious thought.

To his disgust, the driver of the offending car didn't stop, but carried on up the road, took a right and disappeared out of sight.

A passer-by made a tentative approach towards the victim.

'Do not move her,' Francesco barked as he pulled off

his helmet. 'She might have a broken neck. If you want to help, call for an ambulance.'

The passer-by took a step back and dug into his pocket, allowing Francesco to stand over the victim.

The woman lay on her back, half on the pavement and half on the road, her thick hair fanning in all directions. Her helmet, which had shifted forward and covered her forehead, had a crack running through it. Her bike was a crumpled heap of metal.

Dropping to his haunches, Francesco yanked off his leather gloves and placed two fingers on the fallen cyclist's neck.

Her pulse beat faint beneath his touch.

While the passer-by spoke to the emergency services, Francesco deftly removed his leather jacket and placed it over the unconscious woman. She wore smart grey trousers and an untucked black blouse covered with a waterproof khaki jacket. On one of her bare feet was a white ballet shoe. The other was missing.

His chest constricted at the thought of the missing shoe.

He wished he could tuck his jacket under her to create a barrier between her and the cold, damp concrete, but he knew it was imperative to keep her still until the paramedics arrived.

The important thing was she was breathing.

'Give me your coat,' he barked at another spectator, who was hovering like a spare part. A small crowd had gathered around them. Vultures, Francesco thought scornfully. Not one of them had stepped forward to help.

It never occurred to him that his presence was so forbidding, even first thing in the morning, that none of the crowd *dared* offer their assistance.

The spectator he'd addressed, a middle-aged man in

a long lambswool trench coat, shrugged off his coat and passed it to Francesco, who snatched it from his hands. Francesco wrapped it across the woman's legs, making sure to cover her feet.

'Five minutes,' the original passer-by said when he disconnected his call.

Francesco nodded. For the first time he felt the chill of the wind. He palmed the woman's cheek. It felt icy.

Still on his haunches, he studied her face carefully, ostensibly looking for a clue to any unseen injuries. No blood ran from her nose or mouth, which he assumed was a good thing. Her mass of blonde hair covered her ears, so he carefully lifted a section to look. No blood.

As he searched, he noticed what a pretty face she had. Not beautiful. Pretty. Her nose was straight but just a touch longer than the women of his acquaintance would put up with before resorting to surgery. She had quite rounded cheeks, too, something else that would be fixed in the endless quest for perfection. But yes, pretty.

He remembered she'd had something slung around her neck before he'd covered her chest with his jacket. Carefully, he tugged it free.

It was an identity card for one of the hospitals in the capital. Peering closer, he read her name. *Dr H Chapman. Specialist Registrar.*

This woman was a doctor? To his eyes she looked about eighteen. He'd guessed her as a student…

Her eyes opened and fixed on him.

His thoughts disappeared.

Shock rang out from her eyes—and what eyes they were, a moreish hazel ringed with black—before she closed them. When they reopened a few beats later, the shock faded to be replaced by a look of such contentment and serenity that Francesco's heart flipped over.

Her mouth opened. He leaned closer to hear what she had to say.

Her words came out as a whisper. 'So there really is a heaven.'

Hannah Chapman leaned her new bike against the stone building and gazed up at the sparkling silver awning that held one word: *Calvetti's*.

She admired the explicitness of it. This belonged to Francesco Calvetti and no one else.

Even though it was 6:00 p.m. and the club wasn't due to open for another four hours, two hefty-sized men dressed all in black stood beneath the awning, protecting the door. She took this as a good sign—the past three times she'd cycled over, the door hadn't been manned. The club had been empty.

'Excuse me,' she said, standing before them. 'Is Francesco Calvetti in?'

'He's not available.'

'But is he in?'

'He's in but he's not to be disturbed.'

Success! At last she'd managed to track him down. Francesco Calvetti travelled *a lot*. Still, tracking him down was one thing. Getting in to see him was a different matter entirely.

She tried her most winning smile.

Alas, her fake smile wasn't up to par. All it resulted in was the pair of them crossing their arms over their chests. One of them alone would have covered the door. The pair of them standing there was like having a two-man mountain as a barrier.

'I know you don't want to disturb him, but can you please tell him that Hannah Chapman is here to see him?

He'll know who I am. If he says no, then I'll leave, I promise.'

'We can't do that. We have our orders.'

She could be talking to a pair of highly trained SAS soldiers, such was the conviction with which the slightly less stocky of the duo spoke.

Hannah sighed. Oh, well, if it wasn't meant to be, then… so be it.

All the same, she was disappointed. She'd wanted to thank the man personally.

She thrust forward the enormous bunch of flowers and thank-you card. She'd cycled the best part of two miles through London traffic with them precariously balanced in her front basket. 'In that case, could you give these to him, please?'

Neither made a move to take them from her. If anything, their faces became even more suspicious.

'Please? This is the third bunch I've brought for him and I'd hate for them to go to waste. I was in an accident six weeks ago and he came to my rescue and…'

'Wait.' The one on the left cocked his head. 'What kind of accident?'

'I was knocked off my bike by a hit-and-run driver.'

They exchanged glances, then drew back to confer in a language that sounded, to her untrained ear, as if it was Italian. Or she could have imagined it, knowing Francesco Calvetti was Sicilian.

Since she'd discovered the identity of her benefactor, she knew a lot more than she should about Francesco Calvetti. internet searches were wonderful creations. For instance, she knew he was thirty-six, unmarried but with a string of glamorous girlfriends to his name, and that he owned six nightclubs and four casinos across Europe. She also knew his family name was synonymous with the Mafia in Sicily and that his father, Salvatore, had gone by the nickname Sal il Santo—Sal the Saint—a moniker allegedly given due to his penchant for making the sign of the cross over his dead victims.

She wouldn't have cared if his father had been Lucifer himself. It made no difference to what Francesco was—a good man.

The man who'd brought her back to life.

The stockier one looked back to her. 'What did you say your name was?'

'Hannah Chapman.'

'One minute. I will tell him you are here.' He shrugged his hefty shoulders. 'I cannot say if he will speak to you.'

'That's fine. If he's too busy, I'll leave.' She wasn't going to make a scene. She was here to say thank you and nothing else.

He disappeared through the double doors, letting them swing shut behind him.

She hugged the flowers to her chest. She hoped Francesco wouldn't think them pathetic but she hadn't a clue what else she could give him to express her gratitude. Francesco Calvetti had gone above and beyond the call of duty, and he'd done it for a complete stranger.

In less than a minute, the door swung back open, but instead of the bouncer, she was greeted by a man who was—and Lord knew how this was even possible—taller than the guards he employed.

She'd no idea he was so tall.

But then, her only memory of the man was opening her eyes and seeing his beautiful face before her. How clearly she remembered the fleeting certainty that she was dead and her guardian angel had come to take her to heaven, where Beth was waiting for her. She hadn't even been sad about it—after all, who would be upset about being escorted to paradise with the most gorgeous man on either heaven or earth?

The next time she'd opened her eyes she had been in a hospital bed. This time, the fleeting feeling was disappointment she hadn't gone off to paradise with Adonis.

Fleeting feeling? No. It had been more than that. Adonis had come to take her to Beth. To learn she was still alive had been on the verge of devastating. But then, of course, sanity poked through.

As she'd come back to the here and now, and memories of her Adonis kept peppering her thoughts, so, too, came the revelation that she truly was alive.

Alive.

Something she hadn't felt in fifteen years.

Limbo. That was where she'd been. She, hardworking, practical Hannah Chapman, for whom bedtime reading consisted of catching up on medical journals, had been living in limbo.

In the weeks since her accident, she'd convinced herself that her memory of that brief moment was all wrong. No one, surely, could look like he did in her memory and be a mortal? She'd had severe concussion after all. Even the pictures she'd found on the internet didn't do justice to her memory of him.

Turned out her brain hadn't been playing tricks on her.

Francesco Calvetti truly was beautiful...

But in a wholly masculine way.

His tall, lean frame was clothed in tailored dark grey trousers and a white shirt unbuttoned to halfway down his chest, the sleeves rolled up to his elbows. In the exposed V—which she was eye height with—he wore a simple gold cross on a chain, which rested on a dark whorl of hair.

A rush of...*something* coursed through her blood, as if a cloud of heat had been blown through her veins.

Unsettled, Hannah blinked and looked back up at his unsmiling face. Not even the forbidding expression resonating from his deep-set eyes—and what a beautiful colour they were, making her think of hot chocolate-fudge cake—could dent the huge grin that broke out on her face. She extended the flowers and card to him, saying, 'I'm Hannah Chapman and these are for you.'

Francesco looked from the flowers back to her. He made no effort to take them.

'They're a thank you,' she explained, slightly breathless for some reason. 'I know they're a drop in the ocean compared to what you've done for me, but I wanted to get you something to show how grateful I am—I am truly in your debt.'

One of his thick black brows raised and curved. 'My debt?'

A shiver ran up her spine at his deep, accented voice. 'You have done so much for me,' she enthused. 'Even if I had all the money in the world I could never repay you for your kindness, so yes, I am in your debt.'

His eyes narrowed as he studied her a little longer before inclining his head at the door. 'Come in for a minute.'

'That would be great,' she said, not caring in the least that his directive was an order rather than a request.

The two-man mountain that had flanked Francesco up to this point, guarding him as well as they would if she were carrying an Uzi nine-millimetre, parted. She darted between them, following Francesco inside.

After walking through a large reception area, they stepped into the club proper.

Hannah's eyes widened. 'Amazing,' she whispered, turning her head in all directions.

Calvetti's oozed glamour. All deep reds and silver, it was like stepping into old Hollywood. The only club she'd been to was at the age of eighteen when her entire class had descended on The Dell, their sleepy seaside town's only nightclub, to celebrate finishing their A levels. It had been one of the most boring evenings of her life.

Compared to this place, The Dell had been grey and dingy beyond imagination.

And, in fact, compared to Francesco, with his olive skin, short black curly hair and strong jawline, all the men she had ever met in her life were grey and dingy beyond imagination, too.

'You like it?'

Her skin heating under the weight of his scrutiny, she nodded. 'It's beautiful.'

'You should come here one evening.'

'Me? Oh, no, I'm not into clubbing.' Then, fearing she had inadvertently insulted him, quickly added, 'But my sister Melanie would love it here—it's her hen night on Friday so I'll suggest she drops in.'

'You do that.'

It didn't surprise Francesco to learn Hannah Chapman wasn't into clubbing. The women who frequented his clubs were a definite type—partygoers and women looking to hook up with a rich or famous man, preferably both.

Hannah Chapman was a doctor, not a wannabe WAG. He allowed himself to take in her appearance more fully, and noticed that she was dressed professionally, in another variation of the trouser suit she'd been wearing on the day she was knocked off her bike. The lighting in the club had the effect of making her white blouse see-through, illuminating her bra, which, to his trained eye, looked practical rather than sexy. Her thick blonde hair looked as if it hadn't seen a hairbrush in weeks, and he could not detect the slightest trace of make-up on her face.

He'd assumed when he'd seen her at the door that she

had come with an agenda. In his experience, everyone had an agenda.

He slipped behind the bar, watching as she set the flowers and card to one side. He had never been presented with flowers before. The gesture intrigued him. 'What can I get you to drink?'

'I could murder a coffee.'

'Nothing stronger?'

'I don't drink alcohol, thank you. In any case, I've been working since seven and if I don't get an enormous shot of caffeine I might just pass out.' He liked the droll way she spoke, the air of amusement that laced her voice. It made a change from the usual petulant tones he was used to hearing from her sex.

'You're back at work already?'

'I was back within a fortnight, as soon as I'd recovered from the concussion.'

'Any other injuries?'

'A broken clavicle—collarbone—which is fusing back together nicely. Oh, and a broken middle finger, but that seems to be healed now.'

'You don't know if your own finger's healed?'

She shrugged and hopped onto a stool, facing him. 'It doesn't hurt anymore so I assume it's healed.'

'Is that a professional diagnosis?'

She grinned. 'Absolutely.'

'Remind me not to come and see you if I need medical attention,' he commented drily, stepping over to the coffee machine.

'You're about twenty years too old for me.'

He raised a brow.

Her grin widened. 'Sorry, I mean you're twenty years too old for me to treat in a medical capacity, unless you want to be treated on a ward full of babies, toddlers, and kids. I'm specialising in paediatrics.'

It was on the tip of his tongue to ask why she had chosen to specialise in children but he kept his question to himself. He wanted to know why she had sought him out.

He placed a cup in the machine and pressed a button. 'Do you take milk and sugar?'

'No milk but two sugars, please. I might as well overdose on that as well as caffeine.'

His thoughts exactly. He added two heaped spoons to both cups and passed one to her.

His initial assessment of her had been correct. She really was very pretty. Of average height and slender, her practical trousers showcased the most fabulous curvy bottom. It was a shame she was now sitting on it. The more he looked at her, the more he liked what he saw.

And he could tell that she liked what she saw, too.

Yes, this unexpected visit from Dr Chapman could take a nice twist.

A *very* nice twist.

He took a sip of his strong, sweet coffee before placing his cup next to hers, folding his arms across his chest and leaning on the bar before her.

'Why are you here?'

Her eyes never left his face. 'Because I needed to let you know how grateful I am. You kept me warm until the ambulance arrived, then travelled in the ambulance with me, stayed at the hospital for hours until I'd regained consciousness, *and* you tracked down the driver who hit me and forced him to hand himself in to the police. No one has ever done anything like that for me before, and you've done it for a complete stranger.'

Her face was so animated, her cheeks so heightened

with colour, that for a moment his fingers itched to reach out and touch her.

How did she know all this? He'd left the hospital as soon as he'd been given word that she'd regained consciousness. He hadn't seen her since.

'How about you let me buy you dinner one night, so I can thank you properly?' Colour tinged her cheeks.

'You want to buy me dinner?' He didn't even attempt to keep the surprise from his voice. Women didn't ask him out on dates. It just didn't happen. For certain, they thought nothing of cajoling him into taking *them* out to expensive restaurants and lavishing them with expensive clothes and jewellery—something he was happy to oblige them in, enjoying having beautiful women on his arm. But taking the initiative and offering *him* a night out…?

In Francesco's world, man was king. Women were very much pretty trinkets adorning the arm and keeping the bed warm. Men did the running, initially at least, following the traps set by the women so the outcome was assured.

She nodded, cradling her coffee. 'It's the least I can do.'

He studied her a touch longer, gazing into soft hazel eyes that didn't waver from his stare.

Was there an agenda to her surprising offer of dinner?

No. He did not believe so. But Francesco was an expert on female body language and there was no doubt in his mind that she was interested in him.

He was tempted. *Very* tempted.

He'd thought about her numerous times since her accident. There had even been occasions when he'd found his hand on the phone ready to call the hospital to see how she was. Each time he had dismissed the notion. The woman was a stranger. All the same, he'd been enraged to learn the police had failed to track down the man who'd so callously knocked her down. The driver had gone into hiding. Unfortunately for the driver, Francesco had a photographic memory.

It had taken Francesco's vast network precisely two hours to track the driver down. It had taken Francesco less than five minutes to convince the man to hand himself in. By the time he'd finished his 'little chat' with him, the man had been begging to be taken to the police station. Francesco had been happy to oblige.

And now she had come to him.

And he was tempted to take her up on her offer of a meal—not that he would let her pay. It went against everything he believed in. Men took care of their women. The end.

If it was any other woman he wouldn't think twice. But this one was different. For a start, she was a doctor. She was a force for good in a world that was cruel and ugly.

Despite her age and profession, Hannah had an air of innocence about her. Or it could just be that she was totally without artifice. Either way, she had no business getting involved with the likes of him.

If he was a lesser man he would take advantage of her obvious interest, just like his father would have done if he'd been alive.

But he would not be that man. This woman was too... *pure* was the word that came to mind. If she were the usual kind of woman who frequented his world, he would have no hesitation in spelling out how she could repay her so-called debt to him. Naked. And horizontal.

'You owe me nothing,' he stated flatly.

'I do...'

'No.' He cut her off. 'What you consider to be your debt is not redeemable. I did what I did without any thought of payback—consider the fact you are alive and healthy and able to do the job you love to be my payment.'

The animation on her face dimmed a little. 'So you won't let me buy you dinner?'

'Look around you. You don't belong in this seedy world, Dr Chapman. I thank you for taking the time to visit me, but now I have business to attend to.'

'That sounds like a dismissal.'

'I am a busy man.'

Those hazel eyes held his for the longest time before she cast him the most beautiful smile he'd ever been the recipient of, lighting her face into something dazzling.

Then, to his utter shock, Hannah levered herself so her torso was on the bar and pressed her lips to his.

They were the softest of lips, a gentle touch that sent tiny darts fizzing through his blood.

He caught a faint whiff of coffee before she pulled away.

'Thank you. For everything,' she said, slipping back down onto her stool then getting to her feet. Her cheeks glowing, she finished her coffee and reached for her bag, her eyes never leaving his. 'I will never forget what you've done for me, Francesco. You have my undying gratitude.'

As she turned to leave, he called out after her, 'Your sister—she has the same family name as you?'

She nodded.

'I'll leave word that Melanie Chapman's hen party is to be given priority at the door on Friday.'

A groove appeared in her forehead. 'Okay,' she said slowly, clearly not having the faintest idea what he was talking about.

'Your sister will know what it means.' A half smile stole over his face. 'Tell her she'll be on the list.'

'Ah—on the list!' The groove disappeared. Somehow the sparkle in her eyes glittered even stronger. 'I know what *that* means. That's incredibly lovely of you.'

'I wouldn't go that far,' he dismissed, already regretting

his impulsive offer, which had come from where he knew not, but which unsettled him almost as much as her kiss.

Francesco never acted on impulse.

That same serene smile that had curved her cheeks when she'd lain on the road spread on her face. 'I would.'

He watched her walk away, his finger absently tracing the mark on his lips where she'd kissed him.

For the first time in his life he'd done an unselfish act. He didn't know if it made him feel good or bad.

CHAPTER TWO

HANNAH STARED AT the queue snaking all the way round the corner from the door of Calvetti's and sighed. Maybe the queue was an omen to stay away.

No. It couldn't be. Even if it was, she would ignore it. Just being this close to his sanctum was enough to send her pulse careering.

Meeting Francesco in the flesh had done something to her...

'Come on, Han,' her sister said, tugging at her wrist and breaking Hannah's reverie. 'We're on the list.'

'But this is the queue,' Hannah pointed out.

'Yes, but we're *on the list*.' Melanie rolled her eyes. 'If you're on the list you don't have to queue.'

'Really? How fabulous.' She'd thought it meant getting in for free—she had no idea it also encompassed queue jumping.

Giggling, the party of twelve women dressed in black leotards over black leggings, bright pink tutus and matching bunny ears hurried past the queue.

Three men in long black trench coats guarded the door.

Melanie went up to them. 'We're on the list,' she said with as much pride as anyone with a pink veil and bunny ears on her head and the words *Mucky Mel* ironed onto the back of her leotard could muster.

Hannah had guessed Calvetti's was popular but, judging by Melanie's reaction, she could have said she'd got VIP backstage passes to Glastonbury. Her sister had squealed with excitement and promptly set about rearranging the entire evening. Apparently Calvetti's was 'the hottest club in the country', with twice as many people being turned away at the door than being admitted.

Luckily, Melanie had been so excited about it all that she'd totally failed to pump Hannah for information on the man himself. The last thing Hannah wanted was for her sister to think she had a crush on him. It was bad enough knowing her entire family thought she was a closet lesbian without giving them proof of her heterosexuality—one sniff and they'd start trying to marry her off to any man with a pulse.

The bouncer scanned his clipboard before taking a step to one side and unclipping the red cordon acting as a barrier.

'Enjoy your evening, ladies,' he said as they filed past, actually smiling at them.

Another doorman led them straight through to the club, which heaved with bodies and pulsated with loud music, leading them up a cordoned-off set of sparkling stairs.

Her heart lifted to see one of the man mountains who'd been guarding the club the other afternoon standing to attention by a door marked 'Private'.

Surely that meant Francesco was here?

A young hunk dressed in black approached them and led them to a large round corner table. Six iced buckets of champagne were already placed on it.

'Oh, wow,' said Melanie. 'Is this for us?'

'It is,' he confirmed, opening the first bottle. 'With the compliments of the management. If you need anything, holler—your night is on the house.'

'Can I have a glass of lemonade, please?' Hannah asked,

her request immediately drowned out by the hens all badgering her to have one glass of champagne.

About to refuse, she remembered the promise she'd made to herself that it was time to start living.

She, more than anyone, knew how precarious life could be, but it had taken an accident on her bike for her to realise that all she had been doing since the age of twelve was existing. Meeting Francesco in the flesh had only made those feelings stronger.

If heaven was real, what stories would she have to tell Beth other than medical anecdotes? She would have nothing of real *life* to share.

That was something she'd felt in Francesco, that sense of vitality and spontaneity, of a life being *lived*.

Settling down at the table, she took a glass of champagne, her eyes widening as the bubbles played on her tongue. All the same, she stopped after a few sips.

To her immense surprise, Hannah soon found she was enjoying herself. Although she didn't know any of them well, Melanie's friends were a nice bunch. Overjoyed to be given the VIP treatment, they made sure to include her in everything, including what they called Talent Spotting.

Alas, no matter how discreetly she craned her neck, Hannah couldn't see Francesco anywhere. She did, however, spot a couple of minor members of the royal family and was reliably informed that a number of Premier League football players and a world-championship boxer were on the table next to theirs, and that the glamorous women and men with shiny white teeth who sat around another table were all Hollywood stars and their beaus.

'Thank you so much for getting knocked off your bike,' Melanie said whilst on a quick champagne break from the dance floor, flinging her arms around Hannah. 'And thank you for coming out with us tonight and for coming here—I was convinced you were going to go home after the meal.'

Hannah hugged her in return, holding back her confession that she *had* originally planned on slipping away after their Chinese, but that the lure of seeing Francesco again had been too great. It had almost made up for the fact Beth wasn't there to share Melanie's hen night. She wouldn't be there to share the wedding, either.

The wedding. An event Hannah dreaded.

She felt a huge rush of affection for her little sister along with an accompanying pang of guilt. Poor Melanie. She deserved better than Hannah. Since Beth's death, Hannah had tried so hard to be the best big sister they both wished she could be, but she simply wasn't up to the job. It was impossible. How could she be anything to anyone when such a huge part of herself was missing? All she had been able to do was throw herself into her studies, something over which she had always had total control.

But now her drive and focus had been compromised.

Never had she experienced anything like this.

Hannah was a woman of practicality, not a woman to be taken in with flights of fancy. Medicine was her life. From the age of twelve she'd known exactly what she wanted to be and had been single-minded in her pursuit of it. She would dedicate her life to medicine and saving children, doing her utmost to keep them alive so she could spare as many families from the gaping hole that lived in her own heart as she could.

At least, she had been single-minded until a car knocked her off her bike and the most beautiful man in the universe had stepped in to save her.

Now the hole in her heart didn't feel so hollow.

Since that fateful cold morning, her mind had not just been full of medicine. It had been full of *him*, her knight in shining armour, and meeting him in the flesh had only compounded this. She wasn't stupid. She knew she would never fit into his world. His reputation preceded him. Francesco Calvetti was a dangerous man to know and an *exceptionally* dangerous man to get on the wrong side of. But knowing this had done nothing to eradicate him from her mind.

That moment when she'd been lying on the cold concrete and opened her eyes, she had looked at him and felt such warmth.... Someone who could evoke that in her couldn't be all bad. He just couldn't.

'Come on, Han,' said Melanie, tugging at her hand. 'Come and dance with me.'

'I can't dance.' What she really wanted to do was search every nook and cranny of Calvetti's until she found him. Because he was there. She just knew it.

Melanie pointed at the dance floor, where a group of twenty-something men with more money than taste were strutting their stuff. 'Nor can they.'

Francesco watched the images from the security cameras on a range of monitors on his office wall. Through them, he could see everything taking place in his club. The same feeds were piped into the office where his security guys sat holed up, watching the same live images—but the only eyes Francesco trusted were his own. Tomorrow he would head back to Palermo to spot-check his nightclub and casino there, and then he would fly on to Madrid for the same.

A couple of men he suspected of being drug dealers had been invited by a group of city money men into the VIP area. He watched them closely, debating whether to have them dealt with now or wait until he had actual proof of their nefarious dealings.

A sweep of thick blonde hair with pink bunny ears

caught his attention in one of the central feeds. He watched Hannah get dragged onto the dance floor by another pink-tutued blonde he assumed was the hen of said hen party, Melanie.

Not for the first time, he asked himself what the hell Hannah was doing there.

She looked more than a little awkward. His lips curved upwards as he watched her try valiantly to move her body in time to the beat of the music. He'd seen more rhythm from the stray cats that congregated round the vast veranda of his Sicilian villa.

The half smile faded and compressed into a tight line when he read the slogan on her back: Horny Hannah.

That all the hen party had similar personalised slogans did nothing to break the compression of his lips.

It bothered him. Hannah was too...*classy* to have something so cheap written about her, even if it was in jest.

He downed his coffee and absently wiped away the residue on the corner of his lips with his thumb.

What was she doing here? And why did she keep craning her neck as if she was on the lookout for someone?

Since he'd dismissed her three days ago, he'd been unnerved to find her taking residence in his mind. Now was not the time for distractions of any sort, not when the casino in Mayfair was on the agenda. This particular casino was reputed to be one of the oldest—if not *the* oldest—in the whole of Europe. It had everything Francesco desired in a casino. Old-school glamour. Wealth. And credibility. This was a casino built by gentlemen for gentlemen, and while the old 'no women' rule had been relaxed in modern times, it retained its old-fashioned gentility. More than anything else, though, it was the one business his father had wanted and failed to get. This failure had been a thorn in

Salvatore's side until his dying day, when a life of overin-
dulgence had finally caught up with him.

After almost forty years under the sole ownership of Sir
Godfrey Renfrew, a member of the British aristocracy, the
casino had been put up for sale.

Francesco wanted it. He coveted it, had spent two
months charming Godfrey Renfrew into agreeing the sale
of it to him. Such was Godfrey's hatred of Francesco's dead
father, it had taken a month to even persuade him to meet.

What was more, if Francesco's spies were correct, Luca
Mastrangelo was sniffing around the casino, too.

This news meant he absolutely could not afford to lose
focus on the deal, yet still he'd found himself, an hour before opening for the night, giving orders to his hospitality
manager to reserve the best table in the club—for a hen
party of all things. He'd only ever intended to have Melanie Chapman's party on the guest list.

Under ordinary circumstances, free tables were given
to the most VIP of all VIPs and only then because of the
publicity it generated.

He hadn't expected Hannah to be in attendance, but now
she was here he couldn't seem to stop his eyes from flick-
ering to whichever monitor happened to be fixed on her.

Hannah tried heroically to get her feet moving in time with
the music, aware her dancing was easily the least rhythmic of the whole club. Not that this seemed to put any of
the men off. To her chagrin, a few seemed to be suffering
from what her sister termed Wandering Hand Syndrome.
One in particular kept 'accidentally' rubbing against her.
When his hand brushed over her bottom the first time she'd
been prepared to give him the benefit of the doubt, and had
stepped away from him. The second time, when he'd been
bolder and tried to cup her buttocks, she'd flashed him a

smile and said in her politest voice, 'Please don't do that,' he'd removed his hand. Which had worked for all of ten seconds. The third time he groped her, she'd 'accidentally' trod on his foot. And now the sleaze had 'accidentally' palmed her breast and was grinding into her back as if she were some kind of plaything.

Did people actually *like* this kind of behaviour? Did women really find it *attractive*?

Just as she was wishing she had worn a pair of stilettoes like all the other women there so she could bruise him properly, a figure emerged on the dance floor.

Such was Francesco's presence that the crowd parted like the Red Sea to admit him.

Her sister stopped dancing and gazed up at him with a dropped jaw. The other hens also stared, agog, their feet seeming to move in a manner completely detached from their bodies.

And no wonder. A head taller than anyone else on the dance floor, he would have commanded attention even if he'd looked like the back end of a bus. Wearing an immaculately pressed open-necked black shirt and charcoal trousers, his gorgeous face set in a grim mask, he oozed menace.

Even if Hannah had wanted to hide her delight, she would have been unable to, her face breaking into an enormous grin at the sight of him, an outward display of the fizzing that had erupted in her veins.

She'd hoped with a hope bordering on desperation that he would spot her and seek her out, had prepared herself for the worst, but hoped for the best. She'd also promised herself that if he failed to materialise that evening then she would do everything in her power to forget about him. But if he were to appear...

To her disquiet, other than nodding at her without making proper eye contact, his attention was very much focused on the man who'd been harassing her who, despite trying to retain a nonchalant stance, had beads of sweat popping out on his forehead.

Francesco leaned into his face, his nostrils flaring. 'If you touch this woman again, you will answer to me personally. *Capisce?*'

Not waiting for a response, he turned back into the crowd.

Hannah watched his retreating figure, her heart in her mouth.

Melanie shouted over the music to her, her face animated, yet Hannah didn't hear a single syllable.

It was now or never.

Unlike the regularity of her life, where the only minor change to her schedule came in the form of the monthly weekend-night shift, Francesco's life was full of movement and change, hopping from country to country, always seeing different sunsets. Her life was exactly where she had planned it to be and she didn't want to change the fundamentals of it, but there was something so intoxicating about both Francesco and the freedom of his life. The freedom to wake up in the morning and just *go*.

He could go anywhere *right now*.

Hurrying to catch him, she followed in his wake, weaving through the sweaty bodies and then past the VIP tables.

'Francesco,' she called, panic fluttering in her chest as he placed his hand on the handle of the door marked Private.

He stilled.

She hurried to close the gap.

He turned his head, his features unreadable.

The music was so loud she had to incline right into

him. He was close enough for her to see the individual hairs in the V of his shirt and smell his gorgeous scent, all oaky manliness, everything converging to send her pulse racing.

'Why did you just do that?' she asked.

His eyes narrowed, the pupils ringing with intent, before he turned the handle and held the door open for her.

Hannah stepped into a dimly lit passageway. Francesco closed the door, blocking off the thumping noise of the music.

She shook her head a little to try to clear her ringing ears.

He leaned back against the door, his eyes fixed on her.

'Why did you do that?' she repeated, filling the silence with a question she knew he'd heard perfectly well the first time she'd asked it.

'What? Warn that man off?'

'Threaten him,' she corrected softly.

'I don't deal in threats, Dr Chapman,' he said, his voice like ice. 'Only promises.'

'But why?'

'Because he wouldn't take no for an answer. I will not allow abuse of any form to take place on my premises.'

'So you make a point of personally dealing with all unwanted attention in your clubs, do you?'

His eyes bored into hers, his lips a tight line.

Far from his forbidding expression making her turn and run away, as it would be likely to make any other sane person do, it emboldened her. 'And did I really hear you say *capisce*?'

'It's a word that the man will understand.'

'Very Danny DeVito. And, judging by his reaction to it, very effective.'

Something that could almost pass for amusement curled on his lips. 'Danny DeVito? Do you mean Al Pacino?'

'Probably.' She tried to smile, tried hard to think of a witty remark that would hold his attention for just a little longer, but it was hard to think sensibly when you were caught in a gaze like hot chocolate-fudge cake, especially when it was attached to a man as divine as Francesco Calvetti. If she had to choose, she would say the man was a slightly higher rank on the yummy stakes than the cake. And she liked hot chocolate-fudge cake *a lot*, as her bottom would testify.

'Thank you for rescuing me. Again.'

'You're welcome.' He made to turn the door handle. 'Now, if you'll excuse me…'

'Dismissing me again?'

'I'm a very…'

'Busy man,' she finished for him. God, but her heart was thundering beneath her ribs, her hands all clammy. 'Please. I came along tonight because I wanted to see you again. Five minutes of your time. That's all I ask. If at the end of it you tell me to leave then I will and I promise never to seek you out again.'

She held her breath as she awaited his response.

He eyed her coolly, his features not giving anything away, until, just as she feared she was about to run out of oxygen, he inclined his head and turned the handle of another door, also marked Private.

Hannah followed him into a large room that was perhaps the most orderly office she had ever been in. Along one wall were two dozen monitors, which she gravitated towards. It didn't take long to spot her sister and fellow hens, all back at their table, talking animatedly.

It occurred to her that she had simply walked away without telling Melanie where she was going.

'So, Dr Chapman, you wanted five minutes of my time…'

She turned her head to find Francesco staring pointedly at his chunky, expensive-looking watch.

He might look all forbidding but she could sense his curiosity.

How she regretted allowing Melanie to talk her into wearing the 'hen uniform', but it would have been churlish to refuse. She had denied her sister too much through the years. Dressing in a ridiculous outfit was the least she could do. Still, it made her self-conscious, and right then she needed every ounce of courage to say what she needed to say.

She swallowed but held his gaze, a look that was cold yet made her feel all warm inside. Seriously, how could a man with chocolate-fudge-cake eyes be all bad?

'When I was knocked off my bike I thought I'd died,' she said, clasping her hands together. God, but this was so much harder than she had imagined it would be and she had known it would be hard. 'I honestly thought that was it for me. Since then, everything has changed—*I've* changed. My accident made me realise I've been letting life pass me by.'

'How does this relate to me?'

Her heart hammered so hard her chest hurt. 'Because I can't stop thinking about you.'

His eyes narrowed with suspicion and he folded his arms across his chest.

Hannah's nerves almost failed her. Her tongue rooted to the roof of her mouth.

'What is it you want from me?'

Out of the corner of her eye she spotted the thank-you card she'd given him. Seeing it there, displayed on his desk, settled the nerves in her stomach.

Francesco had kept her card.

He'd sought her out and rescued her *again*.

She wasn't imagining the connection between them.

She sucked her lips in and bit them before blurting out, 'I want you to take my virginity.'

CHAPTER THREE

FRANCESCO SHOOK HIS HEAD. For the first time in his thirty-six years he was at a loss for words.

'God, that came out all wrong.' Hannah covered her face, clearly cringing. When she dropped her hands her face had paled but, to give her credit, she met his gaze with barely a flinch. 'I didn't mean it to come out quite so crudely. Please, say something.'

He shook his head again, trying to clear it. 'Is this some kind of joke?'

'No.'

'You're a virgin?'

'Yes.'

For a moment he seriously considered that he was in some kind of dream.

Had he fallen asleep at his desk?

Since the discovery of his mother's diaries ten months ago, he'd been consumed with rage. This rage fuelled him. Indeed, for the past ten months, his drive had been working at full throttle. Only a month ago his doctor had told him to slow down, that he was at risk of burnout. Naturally, he'd ignored that advice. Francesco would not slow down until he had eradicated every last trace of Salvatore Calvetti's empire.

And to think he'd almost missed those diaries. Had he

not given the family home one last sweep before emptying it for sale, he would never have found them, hidden away in boxes in the cubbyhole of his mother's dressing room. He hadn't even intended to go into his mother's rooms but the compulsion to feel close to her one last time had made him enter them for the first time in two decades.

Reading the diaries had been as close to torture as a man could experience. The respect he'd felt for his father, the respect that had made him a dutiful son while his father was alive, had died a brutal death.

His only regret was that he hadn't learned the truth while his father was alive, would never have the pleasure of punishing him for every hour of misery he'd put his mother through. Duty would have gone to hell. He might just have helped his father into an early grave.

He hoped with every fibre of his being that his father *was* in hell. He deserved nothing less.

Because now he knew the truth. And he would not be satisfied until he'd destroyed everything Salvatore Calvetti had built, crushed his empire and his reputation. Left it for dust.

The truth consumed him. His hate fuelled him.

It was perfectly feasible he had fallen asleep.

Except he'd never had a dream that made his heart beat as if it would hammer through his ribcage.

He rubbed the back of his neck and stared at the woman who had made such a confounding offer.

She looked ridiculous in her hen outfit, with the pink tutu, black leotard and leggings, and black ballet slippers. At least the other hens had made an effort, adorning their outfits with the sky-high heels women usually wore in his clubs. It didn't even look as if Hannah had brushed her hair, never mind put any make-up on. What woman went clubbing without wearing make-up?

Indeed, he could not remember the last time he'd met a woman who *didn't* wear make-up, full stop.

And she still had those ridiculous bunny ears on her head.

Yet there was something incredibly alluring about Hannah's fresh-faced looks. Something different.

He'd thought *she* was different. He'd resisted her offer of a date a few short days ago because of it; because he'd thought she was *too* different, that she didn't belong in his world.

Could he really have judged her so wrong?

What kind of woman offered her so-called virginity to a stranger?

And what the hell had compelled him to warn her groper off and not send one of his men in to resolve the situation? If he'd followed his usual procedures he wouldn't be standing here now on the receiving end of one of the most bizarre offers he'd ever heard.

It had been watching that man paw her—and her dignity when rebuffing his advances—that had made something inside him snap.

The rules were the same in all his establishments, his staff trained to spot customers overstepping the mark in the familiarity stakes. The usual procedure was for one of his doormen to have a polite 'word' with the perpetrator. That polite word was usually enough to get them behaving.

Francesco might have little respect for the type of women who usually littered his clubs but that did not mean he would tolerate them being abused in any form.

In the shadows of his memory rested his mother, a woman who had tolerated far too much abuse. And he, her son, had been oblivious to it.

A rush of blood to his head had seen him off his seat,

out of his office and onto the dance floor before his brain had time to compute what his feet were doing.

'I have no idea what you're playing at,' he said slowly, 'but I will not be a party to such a ridiculous game. I have given you your five minutes. It's time for you to leave.'

This *had* to be a game. Hannah Chapman had discovered his wealth and, like so many others of her gender, decided she would like to access it.

It unnerved him how disappointed he felt.

'This isn't a game.' She took a visibly deep breath. 'Please. Francesco, I am a twenty-seven-year-old woman who has never had sex. I haven't even kissed a man. It's become a noose around my neck. I don't want to stay a virgin all my life. All I want is one night to know what it feels like to be a real woman and you're the only man I can ask.'

'But why me?' he asked, incredulous.

Her beautiful hazel eyes held his. 'Because I trust that you won't hurt me.'

'How can you trust such a thing? I am a stranger to you.'

'The only men I meet are fellow doctors and patients. The patients are a big no-no, and the few single doctors I know…we work too closely together. You might be a stranger but I *know* you'll treat me with respect. I know you would never laugh at me or make fun about me being a twenty-seven-year-old virgin behind my back.'

'That's an awful lot of supposition you're making about me.'

'Maybe.' She raised her shoulders in a helpless gesture. 'I thought I was dead. When I opened my eyes and saw your face I thought you'd come to take me to heaven. All I can think now is *what if…* What if I *had* died? I've done *nothing* with my life.'

'Hardly,' he said harshly. 'You're a doctor. That takes dedication.'

'For me, it's taken everything. I'm not naturally bright—I had to work hard to get my grades, to learn and to keep learning. In the process I've been so focused on my career that I've allowed my personal life to go to ruin.' The same groove he remembered from the other evening reappeared on her forehead. 'I don't want to die a virgin.'

Francesco rubbed his neck.

*It seemed s*he was serious.

Of course, she *could* be lying. Having discovered who he was, this could be a clever, convoluted game to access his life and wealth.

Yet her explanation made a mad kind of sense.

He remembered the expression of serenity that had crossed her face at the moment she'd opened her eyes and looked at him, remembered her words and the fuzzy feelings they had evoked in him.

Something had passed between them—something fleeting but tangible.

There was no way Hannah could have known who he was at that moment.

One thing he did know was that she had gained a false impression of him. If she knew who he really was, he would be the last man she would make such a shameless proposition to.

Regardless, he could hardly credit how tempted he was.

He was a red-blooded male. What man *wouldn't* be tempted by such an offer?

But Hannah was a virgin, he reminded himself—despite the fact that he'd thought virgins over the age of eighteen were from the tales of mythology.

Surely this was every man's basest fantasy? A virgin begging to be deflowered.

'You have no idea who I am,' he told her flatly.

'Are you talking about the gangster thing?'

'The gangster thing?' His voice took on a hint of menace. How could she be so blasé about it? Was she so naive she didn't understand his life wasn't something watched from the safety of a television set, played by men who likely had manicures between takes?

Scrutinising her properly, her innocence was obvious. She had an air about her—the same air he saw every time he looked through his parents' wedding album. His mother had had that air when she'd married his father, believing it to be a love match, blissfully oblivious to her husband's true nature, and the true nature of his business affairs.

Hannah raised her shoulders again. 'I've read all about you on the internet. I know what it says your family are.'

'And do you believe everything you read on the internet?'

'No.' She shook her head to emphasise her point.

Deliberately, he stepped towards her and into her space. He brought his face down so it was level with hers. 'You *should* believe it. Because it's true. Every word. I am not a good person for you to know. I am the last person a woman like you should get involved with.'

She didn't even flinch. 'A woman like me? What does that mean?'

'You're a doctor. You do not belong in my world.'

'I just want *one night* in your world, that's all. One night. I don't care what's been written about you. I know you would never hurt me.'

'You think?' Where had she got this ludicrous faith in him from? He had to eradicate it, make her see enough of the truth to scare her all the way back to the safety of her hospital.

He straightened to his full height, an act capable of intimidating even the hardest of men. He breached the inches between them to reach into her thick mane of hair and tug the rabbit ears free. They were connected by some kind of plastic horseshoe that he dropped onto the floor and placed a foot on. He pressed down until he heard the tell-tale crunch.

She stared at him with that same serene look in her hazel eyes.

'Tell me,' he said, gently twisting her around so her back was flush against him, 'how, exactly, do you want me to take your virginity?'

He heard an intake of breath.

Good. He'd unnerved her.

Gathering her hair together, he inhaled the sweet scent of her shampoo. Her hair felt surprisingly soft. 'Do you want me to take you here and now?'

He trailed a finger down her exposed slender neck, over the same collarbone that had been broken less than two months before, and down her toned arm before reaching round to cup a breast flattened by the leotard she wore.

'Or do you want me to take you on a bed?' He traced his thumb over a nipple that shot out beneath his touch.

'I…' Her voice came out like a whimper. 'I…'

'You must have some idea of how you would like me to perform the deed,' he murmured, breathing into her ear and nuzzling his nose into a cheek as soft as the finest silk. 'Is foreplay a requirement? Or do you just want to get it over with?'

'I…I know what you're doing.'

'All I'm doing is ascertaining how, exactly, you would like me to relieve you of your virginity. I can do it now if you would like.' He pressed his groin into the small of her back so as to leave her in no doubt how ready he was. 'Right here, over the desk? Up against the wall? On the floor?'

Much as he hated himself for it, his body was respond-ing to her in the basest of fashions.

He would control it, just as he controlled everything else.

He would *not* give in to temptation.

He would make the good doctor see just how wrong she was about him.

Hannah Chapman was one of the few people in the world who made a difference.

He would not be the one to taint her, no matter how much he desired her or how much she wanted it.

He was better than that. He was better than the man who had created him, who would, no doubt, have already relieved Hannah of her virginity if he'd been in Francesco's shoes.

He would not be that man. And if he had to come on heavy to make her run away, then that was what he would do. Reasoning clearly didn't work with her.

'You're trying to scare me off.'

Francesco stilled at her astuteness.

Although her breaths were heavy, he could feel her defiance through the rigidity of her bones.

It was with far too much reluctance that he released his hold and turned her back round to face him.

Hannah's hair tumbled back around her shoulders. Her cheeks were flushed, her eyes wide. Yet there was no fear. Apprehension, yes, but no fear.

'You are playing with fire, Dr Chapman.'

She gave a wry smile. 'I'm trained to treat burns.'

'Not the kind you will get from me. You'll have to find another man to do the job. I'm not for hire.'

His mind flashed to the man who'd been groping Hannah earlier—who, he imagined, would be more than happy to accede to her request. He banished the image. Who she chose was none of his concern.

All the same, the thought of that man pawing at her

again sent a sharp, hot flush racing through him. She was too...*pure*.

A shrewdness came into her eyes, although how such a look could also be gentle totally beat him.

She tilted her head to the side. 'Do I scare you?'

'On the contrary. It is you who should be afraid of me.'

'But I'm not scared of you. I don't care about your reputation. I'm not after a relationship or anything like that—the only thing being with you makes me feel is good. After everything you've done for me, how can I not trust that?'

He shook his head.

This was madness.

He should call his guards and have her escorted out of his club. But he wouldn't.

Francesco had heard stories about people who saved lives being bound to the person they'd saved, and vice versa. And while he hadn't saved her in a technical sense, it was the only explanation he could think of for the strange chemistry that brewed between them. Total strangers yet inexplicably linked.

Something had passed between them, connecting them.

It was his duty to sever that link. *His* duty. Not his guards'.

He would make her see.

'You think I'm worthy of your trust?' Unthinkingly, he reached out a hand and captured a lock of her hair.

'I *know* you are.' Reclosing the gap between them, she tilted her head back a little and placed a hand on his cheek. 'Don't you see? A lesser man wouldn't try to scare me off—he would have taken what I offered without a second thought'

His skin tingled beneath the warmth of her fingers. He wanted to clasp those fingers, interlace his own through them....

'I'm not cut out for any form of relationship—my career matters too much for me to compromise it—but I want to *feel*.' She brought her face closer so her nose skimmed against his throat, her breath a whisper against his sensitised skin. 'I want one night where I can throw caution to the wind. I want to know what it's like to be made love to and I want it to be you because you're the only man I've met who makes me feel alive without even touching me.'

Francesco could hardly breathe. His fingers still held the lock of her hair. The desire that had been swirling in his blood since he'd nuzzled into her neck thickened.

When had he ever felt as if he could explode from arousal?

This was madness.

'If I believed you felt nothing physically for me, I would walk away now,' she continued, her voice a murmur. 'I certainly wouldn't debase myself any further.'

'How can you be so sure I feel anything for you physically?'

'Just because I'm a virgin doesn't mean I'm totally naive.'

In his effort to scare her away, he'd pressed his groin into her back, letting her feel his excitement through the layers of their clothing.

That particular effort had backfired.

Hannah had turned it round on him.

Well, no more.

Clasping the hand still resting against his cheek, he tugged it away and dropped it. He stepped back, glowering down at her. 'You think you can spend one night with me and walk away unscathed? Because that isn't going to happen. Sex isn't a game, and I'm not a toy that can be played with.'

For the first time a hint of doubt stole over her face. 'I

never meant it like that,' she said, her voice low. 'It's not just that I'm wildly attracted to you, it's more than that. I can't explain it, but when I look at you I see a life full of excitement, of travel, of so much more than I could ever hope to experience. All I want is to reach out and touch it, to experience some of it with you.'

'You think you know me but you don't. I'm not the man you think. My life is seedy and violent. You should want nothing to do with it.'

For long, long moments he eyeballed her, waiting for her to drop her eyes. But it didn't happen—her gaze held his, steady and immovable.

'Prove it.' She gave a feeble shrug. 'If you really think you're so bad for me, then *prove* it.'

He almost groaned aloud. 'It's not a case of proving it. You need to understand—once your virginity's gone you will never get it back. It's lost for ever, and who knows what else you might lose with it.'

She swallowed but remained steady. 'There's nothing else for me to lose. I'm not after a love affair. Francesco, all I want is one night.'

It was hearing his name—and the meaning she put into it—on her lips that threw him.

It made him want to find a dragon to slay just to protect her. Yet he knew that the only thing Hannah needed protecting from was herself.

He reminded himself that he did not need this aggravation. His mind should be focused on the Mayfair deal—the deal that would be the crowning glory in his empire. Hannah had compromised his concentration enough these past few days.

Maybe if he gave her some of what she wanted his mind could regain its focus without her there, knocking on his thoughts.

'You want proof of who I really am?' he said roughly. 'Then that's what you shall have. I will give you a sample of my life for one weekend.'

Her eyes sparkled.

'*This* weekend,' he continued. 'You can share a taste of my life and see for yourself why you should keep the hell away from me. By the end of our time together I guarantee you will never want to see my face again, much less waste your virginity on a man like me.'

CHAPTER FOUR

HANNAH HAD BEEN twitching her curtains for a good half hour before Francesco pulled up outside her house on an enormous motorbike, the engine making enough racket to wake the whole street.

It didn't surprise her in the least that he waited for her to come out to him. Once Francesco had agreed to a weekend together, he had wasted no time in dismissing her by saying, 'I will collect you at 7:00 a.m. Have your passport ready.'

He was taking her to Sicily. To his home.

She couldn't remember the last time she'd been this excited about something. Or as nervous.

Her very essence tingling with anticipation, she stepped out into the early-morning sun, noticing that at least he had taken his helmet off to greet her.

'Good morning,' she said, beaming both at him and, with admiration, at the bike. There was something so...*manly* about the way he straddled it, which, coupled with the cut of his tight leather trousers, sent a shock of warmth right through her. 'Are we traveling to Sicily on this?'

He eyed her coldly. 'Only to the airbase. That's if you still want to come?' From the tone of his voice, there was no doubting that he hoped she'd changed her mind.

If she was honest, since leaving his office six short hours

ago, she'd repeatedly asked herself if she was doing the right thing.

But she hadn't allowed herself to even consider backing down. Because all she knew for certain was that if she didn't grab this opportunity with both hands she would regret it for the rest of her life, regardless of the outcome.

'I still want to come,' she said, almost laughing to see his lips tighten in disapproval. Couldn't he see, the more he tried to scare her off, the more she knew she was on the right path, that it proved his integrity?

Francesco desired her.

The feel of his hardness pressed against her had been the most incredible, intoxicating feeling imaginable. She had never dreamed her body capable of such a reaction, had imagined the thickening of the blood and the low pulsations deep inside were from the realms of fiction. It had only served to increase her desire, to confirm she was following the right path.

She'd been his for the taking in his office but he had stepped back, unwilling to take advantage. Again.

Francesco was doing everything in his power to put her off, but she doubted there was anything to be revealed about him that would do that. What, she wondered, had made him so certain he was all bad? Was it because of his blood lineage? Whatever it was, she knew there was good in him—even though he clearly didn't believe it himself.

Face thunderous, he reached into the side case and pulled out some leathers and a black helmet. 'Put these on.'

She took them from him. 'Do you want to come in while I change? Your bike will be perfectly safe—all the local hoodlums are tucked up in bed.'

'I will wait here.'

'I have coffee.'

'I will wait.'

'Suit yourself.'

'You have five minutes.'

In her bedroom, Hannah wrestled herself into the tight leather trousers, and then donned the matching jacket, staggering slightly under the weight of it.

When she caught sight of her reflection in the full-length mirror she paused. Whoever said leathers were sexy was sorely mistaken—although she'd admit to feeling very Sandra Dee in the trousers.

Sandra Dee had been a virgin, too.

Hannah was a virgin in all senses of the word.

But, she reminded herself, with Francesco's help she was going to change that. Just for this one weekend. That was all she wanted. Some memories to share with Beth.

She took a deep breath and studied her reflection one last time. Her stomach felt knotted, but she couldn't tell if excitement or trepidation prevailed.

She checked the back door was locked one last time before grabbing her small case and heading back out to him.

'That will not fit,' Francesco said when he saw her case.

'You're the one whisking me away for a romantic overnight stay on a motorbike,' she pointed out. 'What do you suggest I do?'

'Let me make this clear, I am not whisking you away anywhere.'

'Semantics.'

'And I never said anything about us going away for one night only. We will return to the UK when *I* am ready.'

'As long as you get me back in time for work at nine o'clock Monday morning, that's fine by me.'

His face was impassive. 'We will return when my schedule allows it, not yours.'

'Is this the part when I'm supposed to wave my hands and say, "oh, in that case I can't possibly come with you?"'

'Yes.'

'Bad luck. I'm coming. And you'll get me back in time for work.'

'You sound remarkably sure of yourself.'

'Not at all. I just know you're not the sort of person to allow a ward full of sick children to suffer from a lack of doctors.'

His features contorted, the chocolate fudge of his eyes hardening. 'That is a risk you are willing to take?'

'No.' She shook her head, a rueful smile playing on her lips. 'I know there's no risk.' At least no risk in the respect of getting her to work on time. And as to Francesco's other concerns, Hannah knew there was no risk in the respect of her heart, either; her heart hadn't functioned properly in fifteen years.

More practically, she supposed there were some dangers. She could very well be getting into something way out of her depth, but what was the worst that could happen? Hannah had lived through her own personal hell. The worst thing that could happen had occurred at the age of twelve, and she had survived it. God alone knew how, but she had.

It was only one weekend. One weekend of *life* before she went back to her patients, the children she hoped with all her semi-functioning heart would grow up to lead full lives of their own.

'On your head be it,' said Francesco. 'Now either find a smaller case for your stuff, put it in a rucksack you can strap to you, or leave it behind.'

Her gaze dropped to her case. She didn't have either a smaller case or a rucksack....

'Give me one minute,' she said, speaking over her shoulder as she hurried back into the house. In record time she'd grabbed an oversized handbag and shoved her passport, phone, purse, clean underwear, toothbrush, and a thin sundress into it. The rest of her stuff, including some research papers she'd been reading through for the past week, she left in the case.

This was an adventure after all. Her first adventure in fifteen years.

'Is that all you're taking?' Francesco asked when she rejoined him, taking the bag from her.

'You're the one who said to bring something smaller.'

He made a noise that sounded like a cross between a grunt and a snort.

She grinned. 'You'll have to try harder than that to put me off.'

Nostrils flaring, he shoved her bag into the side case then thrust the helmet back into her hands. 'Put this on.'

'Put this on…?' She waited for a *please*.

'Now.'

How could *anyone* be so cheerful first thing in the morning? Francesco wondered. It wasn't natural.

What would it take to put a chink in that smiley armour?

With great reluctance, he reached over to help her with the helmet straps. Even through the darkened visor he could see her still grinning.

If he had his way, that pretty smile would be dropped from her face before they boarded his plane.

'Have you ridden on one of these before?' he asked, tightening the straps enough so they were secure without cutting off her circulation.

She shook her head.

'Put your arms around me and mimic my actions—lean into the turns.'

Only when he was certain that she was securely seated did Francesco twist the throttle and set off.

Francesco brought the bike to a halt in the airport's private car park.

'That was amazing!' Hannah said, whipping off her helmet to reveal a head of hair even more tangled than a whole forest of birds' nests.

If his body wasn't buzzing from the exhilaration of the ride coupled with the unwanted thrum of desire borne from having her pressed against him for half an hour, he would think she looked endearing.

His original intention had been to take advantage of the clear early-Saturday-morning roads and hit the throttle. What he hadn't accounted for was the distraction of having Hannah pressed so tightly against him.

And no wonder. Those trousers...

Caro Dio...

Behind that sensible, slightly messy exterior lay a pair of the most fantastic legs he had ever seen. He'd noticed how great they looked the night before, but the ridiculous pink tutu had hidden the best part: the thighs.

Not for a second had he been able to forget she was there, attached to him, trusting him to keep her safe.

Where the hell did she get this misplaced trust *from*?

In the end, he'd kept his speed strictly controlled, rarely breaching the legal limits. Not at all the white-knuckle ride he'd had in mind.

His guards were already there waiting for him, forbidden from following him when he was riding in the UK. It was different on the Med, especially in Sicily. The only good thing he could say about England was he never felt the need to have an entourage watching his back at all times.

In as ungracious a manner as he could muster, he pulled

Hannah's bag from the side case, handed it to her, then threw the keys of his bike to one of his men.

'What are you doing?' he asked, spotting Hannah on her phone. It was one of the latest models. For some reason this surprised him. Maybe it was because she was a virgin who dressed in a basic, functional manner that he'd assumed she'd have a basic, functional phone.

'Answering my emails,' she said, peering closely at the screen as she tapped away.

'From who?'

'Work.'

'It is Saturday.'

She peered up at him. She really did look ridiculous, with the heavy jacket clearly weighing her down. Still, those legs... And that bottom...

'Hospitals don't close for weekends.' She flashed him a quick grin. 'I'll be done in a sec.'

Francesco had no idea why it irked him to witness Hannah pay attention to her phone. He didn't want to encourage her into getting any ideas about them but, all the same, he did *not* appreciate being made to feel second best.

'All done,' she said a moment later, dropping the phone back into her bag.

Once the necessary checks were made, they boarded Francesco's plane.

'You own this?' she asked with the same wide-eyed look she'd had when she'd first walked into his club carrying a bunch of flowers for him.

He jerked a nod and took his seat, indicating she should sit opposite him. 'Before I give the order for us to depart, I need to check your bag.'

'Why? It's already been through a scanner.'

'My plane. My rules.' He met her gaze, willing her to

fight back, to leave, to get off the aircraft and walk away before the dangers of his life tainted her.

He thought he saw a spark of anger. A tiny spark, but a spark all the same.

She shrugged and handed it over to him.

He opened the bag. His hand clenched around her underwear. He should pull it out, let her see him handle her most intimate items. The plane hadn't taken off. There was still time to change her mind.

But then he met her gaze again. She studied him with unabashed curiosity.

No. He would not humiliate her.

His fingers relaxed their grip, the cotton folding back into place. He pulled out a threadbare black purse.

Resolve filled him. He opened it to find a few notes, a heap of receipts, credit and debit cards, and a photo, which he tugged out.

Hannah fidgeted before him but he paid her no heed.

She wanted him to prove in actions how bad he was for her? This was only the beginning.

He peered closely at a picture of two identical young girls with long flaxen hair, hazel eyes, and the widest, gappiest grins he had ever seen.

'You are a twin?' he asked in surprise.

Her answer came after a beat too long. 'Yes.'

He looked at her. Hannah's lips were drawn in. Her lightly tanned skin had lost a little of its colour.

'Why was she not out last night with you, celebrating your other sister's hen night?'

Her hands fisted into balls before she flexed them and raised her chin. 'Beth died a long time ago.'

His hand stilled.

'Please be careful with that. It's the last picture taken

of us together.' There was a definite hint of anxiety in her voice.

This was another clear-cut opportunity to convince her of his true self. All he had to do was rip the photo into little pieces and he guaranteed she would leave without a backward glance.

But no matter how much he commanded his hands to do the deed, they refused.

Hannah's voice broke through his conflicted thoughts. 'Can I have my stuff back now?' she asked, now speaking in her more familiar droll manner.

Without saying a word, he carefully slotted the photo back in its place, blinking to rid himself of the image of the happy young girls.

The last picture of them together?

His stomach did a full roll and settled with a heavy weight rammed onto it.

Getting abruptly to his feet, he dropped the bag by Hannah's seat. 'I need to speak with the crew. Put your seat belt on.'

Hannah expelled all the air from her lungs in one long movement, watching as Francesco disappeared through a door.

There had been a moment when she'd been convinced he was going to crush the photo in his giant hands.

If there was one thing she'd be unable to forgive, it was that.

But he hadn't. He'd wanted to, but the basic decency within him had won out. And he hadn't fired a load of questions about Beth at her, either.

It was very rare that she spoke about her twin. Even after fifteen years, it still felt too raw, as if vocalising it turned it back into the real event that had ripped her apart. People treated her differently. As soon as someone learned about it, she just knew that was how they would start referring to her. *That's the girl whose twin sister died.* She'd heard those very whispers at school, felt the curious glances and the eyes just waiting for the telltale sign of her suffering. She knew what her schoolmates had been waiting for— they'd been waiting for her to cry.

She'd cried plenty, but always in the privacy of her bedroom—the room she'd shared with Beth.

She'd learned to repel the curiosity with a bright smile, and ignore the whispers by burying herself in her school-work. It had been the same with her parents. And Melanie. She'd effectively shut them all out, hiding her despair behind a smile and then locking herself away.

When Francesco reappeared a few minutes later, she fixed that same bright smile on him.

'We'll be taking off in five minutes,' he said. 'This is your last chance to change your mind.'

'I'm not changing my mind.'

'Sicily is my turf. If you come, you will be bound under my directive.'

'How very formal. I'm still not changing my mind.'

His eyes glittered with menace. 'As I said earlier—on your head be it.'

'Gosh, it's hot,' Hannah commented as she followed Francesco off the steps of the plane. She breathed in deeply. Yes, there it was. That lovely scent of the sea. Thousands of miles away, and for a moment she had captured the smell of home. Her real home—on the coast of Devon. Not London. London was where she lived.

'It's summer' came the curt reply.

At least she'd had the foresight to change out of the leathers and into her sundress before they'd landed. Not that Francesco had noticed. Or, if he had, he hadn't acknowledged it, keeping his head buried so deep into what he was doing on his laptop she wouldn't have been surprised if he'd disappeared into the screen. The only time he'd moved had been to go into his bedroom—yes, he had a *bedroom on a plane*!—and changed from his own leathers into a pair of black chinos, an untucked white linen shirt, and a blazer.

A sleek grey car was waiting, the driver opening the passenger door as they approached. Another identical car waited behind, and Francesco's guards piled into it—except one, who got into the front of their own car.

The doors had barely closed before the guard twisted round and handed a metallic grey object to Francesco.

'Is that a gun?' Hannah asked in a tone more squeaky than anything a chipmunk could produce.

He tucked the object into what she assumed was an inside pocket of his blazer. 'We are in Sicily.'

'Are guns legal in Sicily?'

He speared her with a look she assumed was supposed to make her quail.

'I hope for your sake it's not loaded,' she said. 'Especially with you keeping it so close to your heart.'

'Then it's just as well I have a doctor travelling with me.'

'See? I have my uses.'

Despite her flippancy, the gun unnerved her. It unnerved her a lot.

Knowing on an intellectual level that Francesco was dangerous was one thing. Witnessing him handle a gun with the nonchalance of one handling a pen was another.

He's doing this for effect, she told herself. *Remember, this is an adventure.*

'Where are we going?' she asked after a few minutes of silence had passed.

'My nightclub.'

It didn't take long before they pulled up outside an enormous Gothic-looking building with pillars at the doors.

'This is a nightclub?'

'That's where I said we were going.'

In a melee of stocky male bodies, she followed him inside.

The Palermo Calvetti's was, she estimated, at least four times the size of its English counterpart. Although decorated in the same glitzy silver and deep reds and exuding glamour, it had a more cosmopolitan feel.

A young woman behind the bar, polishing all the hardwood and optics, practically snapped to attention at the sight of them.

'Due caffè neri nel mio ufficio,' Francesco called out as he swept past and through a door marked Privato.

Like its English equivalent, his office was spotless. Two of his men entered the room with them—the same two who'd been guarding the English Calvetti's when she had turned up just five short days ago.

Francesco went straight to a small portrait on the wall and pressed his fingers along the edge of the frame until it popped open as if it were the cover of a book.

'Another cliché?' she couldn't resist asking.

'Clichés are called clichés for a reason,' he said with a shrug of a shoulder. 'Why make it easy for thieves?'

Watching him get into his safe, Hannah decided that it would be easier to break into Fort Knox than into Francesco Calvetti's empire. The inner safe door swinging open, her eyes widened to see the sheer size of the space inside, so much larger than she would have guessed from the picture covering it.

Her stare grew wider to see the canvas bags he removed from it and she realised that they were filled with money.

Francesco and his two men conversed rapidly, all the

while weighing wads of notes on a small set of electronic scales and making notes in a battered-looking A4 book. When the young woman came in with two coffees and a bowl of sugar cubes, Francesco added two lumps into both cups, stirred them vigorously, then passed one over to Hannah, who had perched herself on a windowsill.

'Thanks,' she said, ridiculously touched he'd remembered how she liked her coffee.

Not that it would have been hard to remember, she mused, seeing as he took his exactly the same.

The same thought must have run through Francesco's head because his eyes suddenly met hers, a look of consternation running through them before he jerked his head back to what he was doing.

It amazed her that he would allow her in his inner sanctum when such a large amount of money was, literally, on the table. Then she remembered the gun in his jacket, which he had placed over the back of his captain's chair.

Peering less than subtly at his henchmen, she thought she detected a slight bulge in the calf of the black trousers one wore.

Unnerved by the massive amounts of money before her and the fact she was alone in an office with three men, two of whom were definitely armed, she reached for her phone to smother her increasing agitation.

Working through her messages, Hannah's heart sank when she opened an email from an excited Melanie, who had finally, after months of debate, settled on the wedding-breakfast menu. She could only hope the response she fired back sounded suitably enthusiastic, but she couldn't even bring herself to open the attachment with the menu listed on it, instead opening a work-related email.

It was the most significant event in her little sister's life and, much as Hannah wanted to be excited for her, all she felt inside when she thought of the forthcoming day was dread.

'What are you doing?' Francesco asked a while later, breaking through her concentration.

'Going through my messages.'

'Again?'

'I like to keep abreast of certain patients' progress,' she explained, turning her phone off and chucking it back into her bag.

'Even at weekends?'

'*You're* working,' she pointed out.

'This is my business.'

'And the survival and recovery of my patients is *my* business.'

She had no idea what was going on behind those chocolate-fudge eyes but, judging by the set of his jaw and the thinning of his lips, she guessed it was something unpleasant.

A few minutes later and it appeared they were done, the two henchmen having placed all the money into a large suitcase.

'Before you leave for the bank, Mario,' Francesco said, speaking in deliberate English, 'I want you to show the good doctor here your hand.'

The guns hadn't made any overt impression on her, other than what he took to be a healthy shock that he armed himself in his homeland. He felt certain the next minute would change her impression completely.

Mario complied, holding his hand with its disfigured fingers in front of her.

She peered closely before taking it into her own hands and rubbing her fingers over the meaty skin.

A hot stab plunged into Francesco's chest. He inhaled deeply through his nose, clenching his hands into fists.

She was just examining it like the professional she was, he told himself. All the same, even his mental teeth had gritted together.

'What do you see?' he demanded.

'A hand that's been broken in a number of places—the fingers have been individually broken, too, as if something heavy was smashed onto them.'

'An excellent assessment. Now, Mario, I would like you to tell Dr Chapman who broke your hand and smashed your fingers.'

If Mario was capable of showing surprise, he would be displaying it now, his eyes flashing at Francesco, who nodded his go-ahead. This was an incident that hadn't been discussed or even alluded to in nearly two decades.

'Signor Calvetti. He did it.'

Hannah looked up at Francesco. 'Your father?'

Deliberately, he folded his arms across his chest and stretched his legs out. 'No. Not my father.'

Her eyes widened. 'You?'

'*Sì*. I caught him stealing from my father. Take another look at his hand. That is what we do to thieves in my world.'

CHAPTER FIVE

FRANCESCO KEPT HIS gaze fixed on Hannah, waiting for a reaction other than her current open-mouthed horror.

See, he said with his eyes, *you wanted proof? Well, here it is.*

She closed her eyes and shook her head. When she snapped them back open, she gave Mario's hand another close inspection.

'These scars look old,' she said.

'Nearly twenty year,' Mario supplied in his pigeon English. 'Is okay. I ask for it.'

'What—you asked for your hand to be smashed?'

'What he means is that he did the crime knowing what his punishment would be if caught,' said Francesco.

Her eyes shrewd, she nodded. 'And yet, even after what you did to him and his so-called crime, he still works for you, is trusted enough to handle large quantities of money on your behalf, and, if I'm reading this right, carries a gun that he has never turned on you in revenge.'

How did she do it?

She'd turned it round on him *again.*

'Do not think there was any benevolence on my part,' he countered harshly, before nodding a dismissal at Mario, who left the office with his colleague, leaving them alone.

Hannah remained perched on the windowsill, her hair

now turned into a bushy beehive. She'd crossed her legs, her pale blue dress having ridden up her thighs. It was one of the most repulsive articles of clothing he had ever seen: shapeless, buttoned from top to bottom, clearly brought for comfort rather than style. And yet…there was something incredibly alluring about having to guess what lay beneath it….

'What did he steal?'

'He was a waiter at one of my father's restaurants and made the mistake of helping himself to the takings in the till.'

'How much did he take?' she asked. Her former nonchalance had vanished. It pleased him to hear her troubled tone.

'I don't remember. Something that was the equivalent of around one hundred pounds.'

'So you maimed him for one hundred pounds?'

Francesco drew himself to his full height. 'Mario knew the risks.'

'Fair enough,' she said in a tone that left no doubt she meant the exact opposite. 'Why didn't you just call the police?'

'The police?' A mirthful sound escaped from his throat. 'We have our own ways of handling things here.'

'So if he stole from your father, why did *you* mete out the punishment?'

Francesco remembered that day so clearly.

He'd caught Mario red-handed. There had been no choice but to confront him. He'd made him empty his pockets. His father had walked in and demanded to know what was going on.

How clearly he remembered that sickening feeling in the pit of his stomach when Mario had confessed, looking Salvatore square in the eye as he did so.

And how clearly he remembered feeling as if he would

vomit when Salvatore had turned his laser glare to him, his son, and said, 'You know what must be done.'

Francesco had known. And so had Mario, whose own father had worked for Salvatore, and Salvatore's father before him. They'd both known the score.

It was time for Francesco to prove himself a man in his father's eyes, something his father had been waiting on for years. Something *he'd* been waiting on for years, too. A chance to gain his father's respect.

But how could he explain this to Hannah, explain that it had been an opportunity that hadn't just presented itself to him but come gift-wrapped? Refusal had never been an option.

And why did he even care to explain himself?

Francesco didn't explain himself to anyone.

He hadn't explained himself since he'd vomited in the privacy of his bathroom after the deed had been done, and only when he was certain he was out of earshot.

That was the last time he'd ever allowed himself to react with emotion. Certainly the last time he'd allowed himself to feel any vulnerability.

Overnight he'd put his childhood behind him, not that there had been much left of it after his mother had overdosed.

'I did it because it needed to be done and I was the one who caught him.'

She kept her eyes fixed on him. There was none of the reproach or disgust he expected to find. All that was there was something that looked suspiciously like compassion.... 'Twenty years ago you would have been a boy.'

'I was seventeen. I was a man.'

'And how old was he?'

'The same.'

'Little more than children.'

'We both knew what we were doing,' he stated harshly. 'After that night we were no longer children.'

'I'll bet.'

'And how many more hands have you mangled in the intervening years?'

'Enough of them. There are times when examples need to be made.'

Violence had been a part of his life since toddlerhood. His mother had tried to protect him from the worst of his father's excesses but her attempts had not been enough. His first memory was looking out of his bedroom window and witnessing his father beating up a man over a car bonnet. The man had been held down by two of his father's men.

His mother had been horrified to find him looking out and dragged him away, covering his eyes. Francesco had learned only ten months ago that the bruising he often saw on his mother's body was also from the hands of his father, and not the result of clumsiness.

Francesco had spent his entire life idolising his father. Sure, there were things he'd never been comfortable about, but Salvatore was his father. He'd loved and respected him. After his death four years ago, certain truths had been revealed about aspects of his father's business that had taken some of the shine off his memories, like discovering his drug importing. That in itself had been a very bitter blow to bear, had sickened him to the pit of his stomach. But to learn the truth of what he'd done to his mother… It had sent Francesco's world spinning off its axis.

The walls of the spacious office started to close in on him. The air conditioning was on but the humidity had become stifling, perspiration breaking out on his back.

Hannah stared intently into those beautiful chocolate eyes. Only years of practice at reading her patients allowed her to see beneath the hard exterior he projected. There was pain there. A lot of it. 'What is it about me that scares you so much?'

His lips curled into a sneer. Rising from his chair, he strode towards her like a sleek panther. 'You think you scare me?'

'What other reason is there for you to try so hard to frighten me off and go out of your way to try to make me hate you? Because that's what you're doing, isn't it? Trying to make me hate you?'

He stilled, his huge frame right before her, blocking everything else out.

She reached out a hand and placed it on his chest. 'I bet you've never treated a woman like this before.'

'Like what?' he asked harshly, leaning over and placing his face right in hers, close enough for her to feel the warmth of his breath. 'You're the one with the foolish, romanticised notions about me. I warned you from the start that you didn't belong in my world, and yet you thought you knew best.'

'So this is all to make me see the real you?'

'We had a deal, Dr Chapman,' he bit out, grabbing her hand, which still rested against his hard chest, and lacing his fingers through it. He squeezed, a warning that caused no physical pain but was undoubtedly meant to impress upon her that, if he so chose, he *could* hurt her. 'I made you a guarantee that by the end of our time together I would be the last man you would want to give your virginity to.'

Squeezing his fingers in return, her mouth filling with saliva, she tilted her chin a touch. His mouth was almost close enough to press her lips to....

'If you really want to prove it, then hurt me, don't just give me a warning. You're twice my size—it would take no effort for you to hurt me if you really wanted.' Oh, but she was playing with fire. She didn't need Francesco to point that out. But no matter what she had seen in the two hours she'd been in his country, deep in her marrow was the rooted certainty that he would never hurt her, not in any meaningful sense.

If eyes could spit fire, Francesco's would be doing just that. But there was something else there, too, something that darkened as his breathing deepened.

'See?' she whispered. 'You can't hurt me.'

'Where does your faith in me come from?' His voice had become hoarse.

'It comes from *here*,' she answered, pulling their entwined fingers to her chest and pressing his hand right over her heart. 'I've seen the good in you. Why do you have so little faith in yourself?'

'I have no illusions about what I'm like. You have dedicated your life to healing sick children, whereas my life revolves around power and money, and all the seediness they attract.'

'Your power and money mean nothing to me.'

A groan escaped from his lips and he muttered something she didn't understand before snaking his free hand around her neck and pressing his lips to hers.

All the air expelled from her lungs.

She'd had no notion of what kissing Francesco would be like, could never have envisaged the surge of adrenaline that would course through her veins and thicken her blood at the feel of his firm lips hard against hers, not moving, simply breathing her in.

Returning the pressure, she placed a hand to his cheek, kneading her fingers into the smooth skin as she parted her lips and flitted her tongue into the heat of his mouth.

Francesco's breathing became laboured. His hold on her neck tightened then relaxed, the hand held against her chest moving to sweep around her waist and draw her flush against him to deepen the connection. When his own tongue darted into her mouth, she melted into him, two bodies meshed together, kissing with a hunger that bloomed into unimaginable proportions.

He tasted divine, of darkness and coffee and something else Hannah could only assume was *him*, filling her senses.

Deep inside, the pulsations she had first experienced when he had touched her in his London office began to vibrate and hum.

To think she had gone for twenty-seven years without experiencing *this*.

Brushing her hand down his cheek to rest on the sharp crease of his collar, she stroked the tips of her fingers over the strong neck, marvelling at his strength and the power that lay beneath the skin.

It wasn't the power that came from his position in the world that attracted her so much, she thought dimly, it was the latent masculine power within *him*.

Before she could make sense of all the wonderful sensations rising within her, he pulled away—or, rather, wrenched apart the physical connection between them.

His chest rising and falling in rapid motion, Francesco took a step back, wiping his mouth as if to rid himself of her taste.

'I know my power and money mean nothing to you,' he said, virtually spitting the words out. 'That's why getting involved with you is wrong on every level imaginable.'

Trying to clamp down on the humiliation that came hot on the heels of his abrupt rejection, Hannah jumped down from the windowsill. 'I don't know how many times I have to say this, but I do *not* want to become involved with you, not in any real sense. All I want is to experience some of the life every other woman takes for granted but which has passed me by.'

'And you *should* experience it, but it should be with someone who can give you a future.'

'Medicine is my future.'

'And that stops you building a future with a man, does it?'

Not even bothering to hide her exasperation, she shook her head. 'I'm married to my work, and that's the way I like it. I want to make it to consultant level and I've worked too hard and for too long to throw it all away on a relationship that would never fulfil me even a fraction as much as my job does.'

'How can you know that if you've never tried?'

She pursed her lips together. A deep and meaningful debate about her reasons for not wanting a relationship had not been on the agenda. 'I just know, okay?'

'Your job will never keep you warm at night.'

'My hot-water bottle does a perfectly good job of that and, besides, what right do you have to question me on this? I don't see a wedding ring on your finger. If the internet reports on you are true, as you say they are, you seem to have a phobia towards commitment yourself.' Hadn't that been another tick on her mental checklist, the fact Francesco appeared to steer away from anything that could be construed as permanent?

His face darkened. 'I have my reasons for not wanting marriage.'

'Well, I have mine, too. Why can't you respect that?'

Francesco took a deep breath and slowly expelled it. Why could he not just take everything Hannah said at face value? *His* body was telling him to just accept it, to take her back to his villa and take her, just as she'd asked, until she was so sated she would be unable to think.

But even if he did take her words at face value and accepted that she wasn't asking for anything more than one night, it didn't change the fact that making love to her would taint her. She deserved better than Salvatore Calvetti's son, even if she couldn't see it herself.

He would make her see.

'Let's get out of here,' he said, unable to endure the claustrophobia being shut in four walls with Hannah Chapman induced a minute longer. 'I'm taking you shopping.'

'Shopping?'

'You need a dress for tonight.'

'Why? What's happening tonight?'

'We're going to my casino. There's a poker tournament I need to oversee. I'm not having you by my side dressed as some kind of bag lady.'

Her face blanched at his cruel words, but he bit back the apology forming on his tongue.

In truth, there was something unbearably sexy about Hannah's take-me-as-I-am, comfortable-in-my-skin approach to her appearance, and the longer he was in her company, the sexier he found it.

A bag lady.

Francesco looked at her and saw a *bag lady*?

Having been dumped in a designer shop, whereby Francesco had promptly disappeared, leaving at her disposal a driver with the words, 'I'll meet you at my villa in a few hours—buy whatever you want and charge it to me,' Hannah still didn't know whether she wanted to laugh or punch him in the face.

Trying on what was probably her dozenth dress in the plush changing room, she reflected on his words.

Okay, so her appearance had never been a priority, but did she really look like a bag lady?

Her clothes were mostly bought online when the items she already owned started wearing out. She selected clothes based on suitability for work and comfort. Clothes were a means of keeping her body warm.

Her hair… Well, who had the time for regular haircuts? Not hardworking doctors fighting their way up the food chain, that was for sure. And if the rest of her colleagues managed to fit in regular visits to a salon, then good for them. Still, she had to admit her hair had become a little wild in recent years, and racked her brain trying to remember the last time a pair of scissors had been let loose on it. She came up with a blank.

She could remember the first time her mother had let her and Beth go to a proper hairdresser rather than hack at their hair with the kitchen scissors. It had been their twelfth birthday and the pair of them had felt so grown-up. How lovingly they'd attended their hair after that little trip, faithfully conditioning it at regular intervals.

She tried to think of the last time she'd conditioned her hair and came up with another blank.

Was it really possible she'd gone through the past fifteen years without either a haircut or the use of a conditioner? A distant memory floated like a wisp in her memories, of her mother knocking on her bedroom door, calling that it was time for her appointment at the hairdresser's. She remembered the knots that had formed in her throat and belly and her absolute refusal to go.

How could she get a haircut when Beth wouldn't be there to share it with her? Not that she'd vocalised this particular reasoning. She hadn't needed to. Her mother hadn't pressed her on the issue or brought the subject up again. Haircuts, make-up, all the things that went with being a girl on the cusp of womanhood were banished.

How had she let that happen?

After selecting a dress, a pair of shoes and matching clutch, and some sexy underwear which made her blush as she fingered the silken material, she handed the items to the manager, along with her credit card.

'Signor Calvetti has made arrangements to pay,' the manager said.

'I know, but I can pay for my own clothes, thank you.'

'It is very expensive.'

'I can afford it.' And, sadly, she could. She didn't drink and rarely socialised—Melanie's hen do had been Hannah's first proper night out that year. After paying off her mortgage and other household bills every month, her only expenditure was food, which, when you were buying frozen meals for one, didn't amount to much. She didn't drive. Her only trips were her monthly visits to her parents' home in Devon, for which she always got a lift down with Melanie and her soon-to-be brother-in-law.

Her colleagues, especially those around the same age as her, regularly complained of being skint. Hannah, never spending any money, had a comfortable nest egg.

How had she allowed herself to get in this position?

It was one thing putting money aside for a rainy day but, quite frankly, she had enough stashed away that she could handle months of torrential rain without worrying.

Despite her assurance, the store manager still seemed reluctant to take her card.

'Either accept my card or I'll find a dress in another shop,' Hannah said, although not unkindly. She smiled at the flustered woman. 'Honestly, there's enough credit on there to cover it.'

'But Signor Calvetti…'

Ah. The penny dropped. It wasn't that the manager was worried about Hannah's credit; rather, she was worried about what Francesco would do when he learned his wishes had been overruled. 'Don't worry about him—I'll make sure he knows I insisted. He's learning how stubborn I can be in getting my own way.'

With great reluctance, the manager took Hannah's card. Less a minute later the purchase was complete. Hannah had spent more in one transaction than she'd spent on her entire wardrobe since leaving medical school.

'I don't suppose you know of a decent hairdresser that could fit me in with little notice, do you?'

The manager peered a little too closely at Hannah's hair, a tentative smile forming on her face. 'For Signor Calvetti's lover, any salon in Palermo will fit you in. Would you like me to make the phone call?'

Signor Calvetti's lover... Those words set off a warm feeling through her veins, rather as if she'd been injected with heated treacle. 'That's very kind, thank you—I'll be sure to tell Francesco how helpful you've been.'

Five minutes later Hannah left the boutique with a shop assistant personally escorting her to the selected salon, her driver/bodyguard trailing behind them.

Having her hair cut was one of the most surreal events she could ever recall and, considering the dreamlike quality of the day thus far, that was saying something.

The salon itself was filled with women who were clearly the cream of Sicilian society, yet Hannah was treated like a celebrity in her own right, with stylists and assistants fawning all over her and thrusting numerous cups of strong coffee into her hands.

At the end, when she was given the bill, she made an admirable job of not shrieking in horror.

Oh, well, she told herself as she handed her credit card over for another battering, it would surely be worth it.

She was determined that, after tonight, Francesco would never look at her like a bag lady again.

CHAPTER SIX

HANNAH HAD BEEN shopping in Palermo for such a long time that Francesco started to think she'd had second thoughts and hopped on a plane back to London.

He could have found out for himself by calling the bodyguard he'd left to watch over her, but resisted each time the urge took him. He'd stopped himself making that call for almost two hours.

Thus, when the bulletproof four-by-four pulled up within the villa's gates late afternoon, he fully expected Hannah to get out laden with bags and packages, having gone mad on his credit card. Likely, she would have changed into one of her new purchases.

Instead, she clambered her way out and up the steep steps leading to the main entrance of his villa, still dressed in that ugly shapeless dress. All she carried was her handbag and two other bags and, to top it all off, she wore a navy blue scarf over her hair.

She looked a bigger mess than when he'd left her in the boutique.

Even so, his heart accelerated at the sight of her.

Taking a deep breath to slow his raging pulse, then another when the first had zero effect, Francesco opened his front door.

Hannah stood on the step before him. 'This is your home?' she asked, her eyes sparkling.

'*Sì.*'

'It's fabulous.'

It took every ounce of restraint within him not to allow his lips to curve into the smile they so wanted. 'Thank you.'

He took a step back to admit her. 'You were a long time.' Immediately he cursed himself for voicing his concern.

'The boutique manager—a fabulous woman, by the way—managed to get me into a hairdresser's.'

'You've had your hair cut?' He caught a whiff of that particular scent found only in salons, a kind of fragrant chemical odour. It clung to her.

'Kind of.' Her face lit up with a hint of mischief. 'You'll just have to wait and see—the hairdresser wrapped the scarf round it so it didn't get wind damaged or anything.' She did a full three-sixty rotation. 'I can't believe this is your home. Do you live here alone?'

'I have staff, but they live in separate quarters.'

'It's amazing. Really. Amazing.'

Francesco's home was a matter of pride, his sanctuary away from a life filled with hidden dangers. Hannah's wide-eyed enthusiasm for it filled his chest, making it expand.

'Who would have guessed being a gangster would pay so well?' Her grin negated the sting her words induced. 'I'm just saying.' She laughed, noticing his unimpressed expression. 'You're the one trying to convince me you're a gangster.'

'You really don't believe in beating around the bush, do you?'

Her nose scrunched up a little. 'Erm...I guess not. I've never really thought about it.'

'It's very refreshing,' he surprised himself by admitting.

'Really? And is that a good thing?'

'Most refreshing things are good.'

'In that case…excellent. It's nice to know there's something about me you approve of.' Despite the lightness of her tone, he caught a definite edge to it, an edge he didn't care for and that made him reach over and grab her wrist.

'When are you going to learn, Dr Chapman, that my approval should mean nothing to a woman like you?'

'And when are you going to learn, Signor Calvetti, that I may be a doctor but I am still a human being? I am still a woman.'

He was now certain the edge he had detected was the whiff of reproach.

Surely he should be delighted she was starting to see through the layers to the real man inside. So why did he feel more unsettled than ever?

'Believe me, *Dr* Chapman,' he said, putting deliberate emphasis on her title, 'I am well aware that beneath your haphazard appearance is a woman.'

A smile flitted over her face, not the beaming spark of joy he was becoming accustomed to but a smile that could almost be described as shy. Bright spots of colour stained her cheeks.

Shoving his hands in his pockets lest they did something stupid like reach out for her again, Francesco inclined his head to the left. 'If you head in that direction you will go through several living rooms before you reach the indoor pool, which you are welcome to use, although you might prefer the outside one. If you go through the door on the other side of the pool you'll find the kitchen. If you're hungry my chef will cook something for you, but I would suggest you keep it light as we will be dining in the casino.'

'We're eating out?'

'Yes. I'll show you to the room you will be sleeping in whilst you're here as my guest.'

'Which is only until tomorrow,' Hannah stated amiably, biting back the question of whether it would be *his* room she would be sleeping in, already knowing the answer.

Francesco's villa was a thing of beauty, a huge white palace cleverly cut into the rocks of the hillside. Walking up the steps to his home, the scent of perfumed flowers and lemons had filled her senses so strongly she would have been happy to simply stand there and enjoy. If she hadn't been so keen to see Francesco, she would have done.

She'd been aware he possessed great wealth, but even so...

It felt as if she'd slipped through the looking glass and landed in a parallel universe.

She followed him through huge white arches, over brightly coloured tiled flooring, past exotic furniture, and up a winding stone staircase to a long, uneven corridor.

'Was this once a cave?' she asked.

He laughed. *Francesco actually laughed.* It might not have been a great big boom echoing off the high ceilings, more of a low chuckle, but it was a start and it made her heart flip.

'Its original history is a bit of a mystery,' he said, opening a door at the end of the corridor. 'This is your room.'

Hannah clamped a hand over her mouth to stop the squeal that wanted to make itself heard. Slowly she drank it all in: the four-poster bed, the vibrant colours, the private balcony overlooking the outdoor pool...

'Wow,' she said when she felt capable of speaking without sounding like a giddy schoolgirl. 'If I didn't have to get back to work on Monday, I'd be tempted to claim squatters' rights.'

'You're still trusting I will get you back to London in time?'

She rolled her eyes in answer.

'Let us hope your faith in me is justified.'

'If I turn out to be wrong then no worries—I'll get my own flight back.'

'And what about your passport? You will need that to leave the country.'

'My passport's in my bag.'

'You are sure about that?' At her puzzled expression, Francesco leaned over and whispered into her ear, 'A word of advice, Dr Chapman—when in the company of criminals, never leave your bag open with your passport and phone in it.'

With that, he strolled to the door, patting his back pocket for emphasis. 'Be ready to leave in two hours.'

Hannah watched him close the door before diving into her handbag.

Unbelievable! In the short time she'd been in his home, Francesco had deftly removed her passport and mobile and she hadn't noticed a thing.

She should be furious. She should be a lot of things. He had her passport—effectively had her trapped in his country— but it was her phone she felt a pang of anxiety over.

She had to give him points for continuing to try to make her see the worst in him, but there was no way in the world he would keep hold of her stuff. She had no doubt that, come the morning, he would return the items to her.

The morning…

Before the morning came the night.

And a shiver zipped up her spine at the thought of what that night could bring.

Francesco sat on his sprawling sofa catching up on the day's qualifying event for one of the many motor racing sports he followed, when he heard movement behind the archway dividing the living room from the library.

Sitting upright, he craned his neck to see better.

He caught a flash of blue that vanished before reappearing with a body attached to it. Hannah's body.

Hannah's incredible body.

His jaw dropped open.

There she stood, visibly fighting for composure, until she expanded her arms and said, 'What do you think? Do I still resemble a bag lady?'

A bag lady? He could think of a hundred words to describe her but the adjective that sprang to the forefront of his mind was *stunning*.

Where the blue dress she had changed into on his plane had been a drab, ill-fitting creation, this soft blue dress was a million miles apart. Silk and Eastern in style with swirling oriental flowers printed onto it, it skimmed her figure like a caress, landing midthigh to show off incredibly shapely legs.

Whatever the hairdresser had been paid could never be enough. The thick mop of straw-like hair had gone. Now Hannah's hair was twisted into a sleek knot, pinned in with black chopsticks. There was not a millimetre of frizz in sight. If his eyes were not deceiving him, she'd had colour applied to it, turning her multicoloured locks into more of a honey blonde.

She wore make-up, too, her eyes ringed with dark smokiness that highlighted the moreish hazel, her lips a deep cherry-red...

She looked beautiful.

And yet...

He hated it.

She no longer looked like Hannah.

'No. You no longer resemble a bag lady.'

'Well, that's a relief.' She shuffled into the room on shoes with heels high enough to make her hobble—although not as high as many women liked to wear—and stood before him, her hand outstretched. Her short nails hadn't been touched, a sight he found strangely reassuring. 'Can I have my phone back, please?'

'You can have it back when you leave Sicily.'

'I'd like it back now.'

'For what reason?'

'I've told you—I like to keep abreast of what's going on with my patients.'

'And what can you do for them here?'

'Not worry about them. No news is good news.'

'Then it seems I am doing you a favour.'

'But how am I going to know if there is no news? Now I'll worry that bad news has come and I won't know one way or the other.'

Hiding his irritation, he said, 'Do all doctors go to such lengths for their patients?'

Her lips pressed together. 'I have no idea. It's none of my concern what my colleagues get up to when they're off duty.'

'What happened to professional detachment? I thought you doctors were trained to keep your distance?'

A hint of fire flashed in her eyes. 'Keeping a check on the welfare of my patients is at odds with my professionalism?'

'I'm just asking the question.'

'Well, don't. I will not have my professionalism questioned by you or anyone.'

It was the first time Francesco had heard her sound even remotely riled. He'd clearly hit a nerve.

Studying her carefully, he got to his feet. 'I think it will do you good to spend one evening away from your phone.'

Hannah opened her mouth to argue but he placed a finger to it. 'I did not mean to question your professionalism. However, I am not prepared to spend the evening with someone who has only half a mind on what's going on. Constantly checking your phone is rude.'

Her cheeks heightened with colour, a mutinous expression blazing from her eyes.

'I will make a deal with you,' he continued silkily. 'You say you want to experience all the world has to offer, yet it will be a half-hearted experience if you are preoccupied with worrying about your patients. If you prove that you can let your hair down and enjoy the experience of what the casino has to offer, I will give you your phone back when we return to the villa.'

For the first time since she'd met him, Hannah wanted to slap Francesco. Okay, keep her passport until it was time to leave—that didn't bother her. She knew she would get it back. She knew she would get her phone back eventually, too, but she needed it *now*. She needed to keep the roots the mobile gave her to the ward.

And how dared he imply that she had no detachment? She had it. But she refused to lose her empathy. Her patients were her guiding motive in life. Never would she allow one of her young charges to be on the receiving end of a doctor who had lost basic humanity. She wouldn't. She couldn't. She'd been at the other end and, while it hadn't made the pain of what she went through any worse, a little compassion would have helped endure it that little bit better.

Eventually she took a deep breath and bestowed Francesco with her first fake smile. 'Fine. But if you want me to let my hair down and enjoy myself it's only fair you do the same, too. After all,' she added airily, 'I would say that, of the two of us, you're the greater workaholic. At least I take weekends off.'

Calvetti's casino was a titanic building, baroque in heritage, set over four levels in the heart of Palermo. Hannah followed Francesco up the first sweeping staircase and into an enormous room filled with gambling tables and slot machines as far as the eye could see. It was like stepping into a tasteful version of Vegas.

Flanked by his minders, they continued up the next set of stairs to the third floor. There, a group of men in black parted to admit them into a room that seemed virtually identical to the second floor. It took a few moments for her to realise what the subtle differences were. The lower level was filled with ordinary punters. The third floor, which had around a quarter of the number of customers, was evidently the domain of the filthy rich.

Sticking closely to Francesco, Hannah drank everything in: the gold trimming on all the tables, the beautiful fragrant women, the men in tuxedos—which, she noted, none filled as well as Francesco, who looked even more broodingly gorgeous than usual in his. After a host of conversations, Francesco slipped an arm around her waist and drew her through a set of double doors and into the restaurant.

And what a restaurant it was, somehow managing to be both opulent and elegant.

'Are the customers on the second floor allowed to dine in here?' she asked once they'd been seated by a fawning maître d' at a corner table.

'They have their own restaurant,' he said, opening his leather-bound menu.

'But are they allowed to eat in here?'

'The third floor is for private members only. Anyone can join, providing they can pay the fifty thousand euro joining fee and the ten thousand annual membership.'

She blinked in shock. 'People pay that?'

'People pay for exclusivity—the waiting list is longer than the actual membership list.'

'That's mind-blowing. I feel like a gatecrasher.'

She only realised he'd been avoiding her stare when he raised his eyes to look at her.

'You are with me.'

The possessive authority of his simple statement set her pulse racing, and in that moment she forgot all about being mad at him for refusing to hand back her phone.

'So what do you recommend from the menu?' she asked when she was certain her tongue hadn't rooted to the roof of her mouth.

'All of it.'

She laughed, a noise that sounded more nervous than merry.

A waiter came over to them. *'Posso portarti le bevande?'*

Francesco spoke rapidly back to him.

'He wanted our drink order,' he explained once the waiter had bustled off. 'I've ordered us a bottle of Shiraz.'

'Is that a wine?'

'Yes. The Shiraz we sell here is of the highest quality.'

'I don't drink wine. I'll have a cola instead.'

A shrewdness came into his eyes. 'Have you ever drunk wine?'

'No.'

'Have you ever drunk alcohol?'

'I had a few sips of champagne at Mel's hen do.' Suddenly it occurred to her that Melanie's hen party had been just twenty-four hours ago.

Where had the time gone?

It felt as if she'd experienced a whole different life in that short space of time.

'And that was your first taste of alcohol?'

She stared at him, nodding slowly, her mind racing. After all, wasn't the whole point of her being in Sicily with Francesco to begin her exploration of life? 'Maybe I *should* have a glass of the Shiraz.'

He nodded his approval. 'But only a small glass. Your body has not acquired a tolerance for alcohol.'

'My body hasn't acquired a tolerance for anything.'

The waiter returned with their wine and a jug of water before Francesco could ask what she meant by that comment.

The more time he spent with Hannah, the more intriguing he found her. Nothing seemed to faze her, except having her professionalism cast into doubt. And having her phone taken away.

He watched as she studied the menu, her brow furrowed in concentration. 'Are mussels nice?' she asked.

'They're delicious.'

She beamed. 'I'll have those, then.'

A platter of antipasto was brought out for them to nibble on while they waited for their meals to be cooked.

'Is this like ham?' she asked, holding up a slice of prosciutto.

'Not really. Try some.'

She popped it into her mouth and chewed, then nodded her approval. Swallowing, she reached for a roasted pepper.

'Try some wine,' he commanded.

'Do I sniff it first?'

'If you want.' He smothered a laugh when she practically dunked her nose into the glass.

She took the tiniest of sips. 'Oh, wow. That's really nice.'

'Have you really never drunk wine before?'

'I really haven't.' She popped a plump green olive into her mouth.

'Why not?'

Her nose scrunched. 'My parents aren't drinkers so we never had alcohol in the house. By the time I was old enough to get into experimenting I was focused on my studies. I wasn't prepared to let anything derail my dream of being a doctor. It was easier to just say no.'

'How old were you when you decided to be a doctor?'

'Twelve.'

'That's a young age to make a life-defining choice.'

'Most twelve-year-olds have dreams of what they want to do when they grow up.'

'Agreed, but most change their mind.'

'What did you want to be when *you* were twelve?'

'A racing bike rider.'

'I can see you doing that,' she admitted. 'So what stopped you? Or did you just change your mind?'

'It was only ever a pipe dream,' he said with a dismissive shrug. 'I was Salvatore Calvetti's only child. I was groomed from birth to take over his empire.'

'And how's that going?'

Francesco fixed hard eyes on her. 'I always knew I would build my own empire. I am interested to know, though, what drew you to medicine in the first place—was it the death of your sister?'

A brief hesitation. 'Yes.'

'She was called Beth?'

Another hesitation followed by a nod. When Hannah reached for her glass of water he saw a slight tremor in her hand. She took a long drink before meeting his eyes.

'Beth contracted meningitis when we were twelve. They said it was flu. They didn't get the diagnosis right until it was too late. She was dead within a day.'

She laid the bare facts out to him in a matter-of-fact manner, but there was something in the way she held her poise that sent a pang straight into his heart.

'So you decided to be a doctor so you could save children like Beth?'

'That's a rather simplistic way of looking at it, but yes. I remember walking through the main ward and going past cubicles and private rooms full of ill children and their terrified families, and I was just full of so much... Oh, I was full up of every emotion you could imagine. Why her? Why not me too? Meningitis is so contagious....' She took a deep breath. 'I know you must think it stupid and weak, but when Beth died the only thing that kept me going was the knowledge that one day I would be in a position to heal as many of those children as I could.'

Francesco expelled a breath, the pang in his heart tightening. 'I don't think it's weak or stupid.'

Hannah took another sip of her water. The tremor in her hand had worsened and he suddenly experienced the strangest compulsion to reach over and squeeze it.

'My mother was hospitalised a number of times—drug overdoses,' he surprised himself by saying. 'It was only the dedication of the doctors and nurses that saved her. When she died it was because she overdosed on a weekend when she was alone.'

He still lived with the guilt. On an intellectual level he knew it was misplaced. He'd been fifteen years old, not yet a man. But he'd known how vulnerable his mother was and yet still he and his father had left her alone for the weekend, taking a visit to the Mastrangelo estate without her.

It had ostensibly been for business, his father and Pietro Mastrangelo close friends as well as associates. At least, they had been close friends then, before the friendship between the Calvettis and Mastrangelos had twisted into antipathy. Back then, though, Francesco had been incredibly proud that his father had wanted him to accompany him, had left with barely a second thought for his mother.

While Francesco and Salvatore had spent the Saturday evening eating good food, drinking good wine and playing cards with Pietro and his eldest son, Luca, Elisabetta Calvetti had overdosed in her bed.

To think of his mother dying while he, her son, had been basking in pride because the monster who fed her the drugs had been treating him like a man…. To think that bastard's approval ever meant anything to him made his stomach roil violently and his nails dig deep into his palms.

His mother had been the kindest, most gentle soul he had ever known. Her death had ripped his own soul in half. His vengeance might be two decades too late, but he would have it. Whatever it took, he would avenge her death and throw the carcass of his father's reputation into the ashes.

'I have nothing but the utmost respect for medical professionals,' he said slowly, unfurling the fists his hands had balled into, unsure why he was confiding such personal matters with her. 'When I look at you, Dr Chapman, I see a woman filled with compassion, decency, and integrity. The world I inhabit is driven by money, power, and greed.'

'You have integrity,' she contradicted. 'A whole heap of it.'

'On that we will have to disagree.' He nodded towards the waiter heading cautiously towards them. 'It looks as if our main courses are ready. I suggest we move on from this discussion or both our meals will be spoiled.'

She flashed him a smile of such gratitude his entire chest compressed tightly enough that for a moment he feared his lungs would cease to work.

CHAPTER SEVEN

THANKFULLY, FRANCESCO KEPT the conversation over the rest of their meal light, with mostly impersonal questions about medical school and her job. His interest—and it certainly seemed genuine—was flattering. In turn, he opened up about his love of motorbikes. It didn't surprise her to learn he owned a dozen of them.

When their plates were cleared and Hannah had eaten a dark-chocolate lava cake, which was without doubt the most delicious pudding she'd ever eaten—except hot chocolate-fudge cake, of course—Francesco looked at his watch. 'I need to check in with my head of security before the poker tournament starts. Do you want to come with me or would you like me to get one of my staff to give you a tour of the tables?'

'Are you entering the tournament?'

'No. This one is solely for members. It's the biggest tournament that's held here, though, and the members like to see me—it makes them feel important,' he added, and she noticed a slight flicker of amusement in his eyes, which made her feel as if she'd been let into a private joke. It was an insight that both surprised and warmed her.

'You don't have much time for them?'

'I always make time for them.'

'That's not what I meant.'

'I know what you meant.' His lips, usually set in a fixed line, broke into something that almost resembled a lazy smile. He drained his glass of wine, his eyes holding firm with hers. 'Do you know the rules of poker?'

'Funnily enough, I do. It's often on late at night when I'm too brain-dead to study any longer and need to wind down before bed.'

'You're still studying?'

'Yes. Plus there are always new research papers being published and clinical studies to read through and mug up on.'

'Doesn't sound as if you leave yourself any time for having fun,' he remarked astutely.

'It's fun to me. But you're right—it's why I'm here after all.'

'When you said you'd spent your whole adult life dedicating yourself to medicine, I didn't think you meant it in a literal sense.'

She shrugged and pulled a face. 'It's what I needed.'

'But that's changed?'

'Not in any fundamental way. Medicine and my patients will always be my first priority, but my accident… It made me open my eyes…' Her voice trailed away, unexpected tears burning the back of her eyes. It had been so long since she'd spoken properly about Beth.

Hannah carried her sister with her every minute of every day, yet it had felt in recent weeks as if she were right there with her, as if she could turn her head and find Beth peering over her shoulder.

Blinking back the tears, she spoke quietly. 'I don't know if heaven exists, but if it does, I don't want Beth to be angry with me. She loved life. We both did. I'd forgotten just how much.'

She almost jumped out of her seat when Francesco placed a warm hand on hers, so large it covered it entirely. A sense of calm trickled through her veins, while conversely her skin began to dance.

'Would you like to enter the poker tournament?'

'Oh, no, I couldn't.'

'Think of the experience. Think of the story you'll have to tell Beth.'

With a stab, she realised how carefully he'd been listening. Francesco understood.

The sense of calm increased, settling into her belly. 'Well...how much does it cost?'

'For you, nothing. For everyone else, it's one hundred thousand euros.'

If her jaw could thud onto the table, it would. 'For one game of poker?'

'That's pocket change to the members here. People fly in from all over the world for this one tournament. We allow sixty entrants. We've had a couple drop out, so there is room for you.'

'I don't know. Won't all the other entrants be cross that I'm playing for free?'

'They wouldn't know. In any case, it is none of their business. My casino, my rules. Go on, Hannah. Do it. Enjoy yourself and play the game.'

It was the first time he'd addressed her by her first name. Oh, but it felt so wonderful to hear her name spilling from his tongue in that deep, seductive accent.

Play the game.

It had been fifteen years since she'd played a game of any sort—and school netball most certainly did *not* count when compared to this.

Straightening her spine, she nodded, a swirl of excitement uncoiling in her stomach. 'Go on, then. Sign me up.'

* * *

Francesco watched the tournament unfold from the sprawling security office on the top floor of the casino, manned by two dozen staff twenty-four hours a day. Other than the bathrooms, there wasn't an inch of the casino not monitored. Special interest was being taken in a blackjack player on the second floor—a man suspected of swindling casinos across the Continent. Of course, there was the option to simply ban the man from the premises, but first Francesco wanted proof. And banning was not enough. Once his guilt was established, a suitable punishment would be wrought.

The first round of the tournament was in full swing. On Hannah's table of six, two players were already out. Her gameplay surprised him—for a novice, she played exceptionally well, her poker face inscrutable. Of those remaining, she had the second-largest number of chips.

The dealer dealt the four players their two cards and turned three over on the table. From his vantage point, Francesco could see Hannah had been dealt an ace and a jack, both diamonds. The player with the largest pile of chips had been dealt a pair of kings. One of the table cards was a king, giving that player three of a kind. The player went all in, meaning that if Hannah wanted to continue playing she would have to put *all* her remaining chips into the pile.

She didn't even flinch, simply pushed her pile forward to show she wanted to play.

There was no way she could win the hand. Lady Luck could be kind, but to overturn a three of a kind... The next table card to be turned over was an ace, quickly followed by another ace.

She'd won the hand!

It seemed that fifteen years of perfecting a poker face,

along with too many late nights half watching the game played out for real on the television had paid off.

Hannah allowed herself a sip of water but kept her face neutral. The game wasn't over yet. No one looking at her would know the thundering rate of her heart.

The look on her defeated opponent's face was a picture. He kept staring from his cards to hers as if expecting a snake to pop out of them. Her two remaining opponents were looking at her with a newfound respect.

If she wasn't in the midst of a poker tournament, she'd be hugging herself with the excitement of it all. It felt as if she were in the middle of a glamorous Hollywood film. All that was needed was for the men to light fat cigars and create a haze of smoke.

As the next hand was dealt she noticed a small crowd forming around their table and much whispering behind hands.

She looked at her two cards and raised the ante. One of her opponents matched her. The other folded, opting to sit out of the hand. The table cards were laid. Again she raised the ante. Again her opponent matched her. And so it went on, her opponent matching her move for move.

She didn't have the best of hands: two low pairs. There was every chance that his cards were much better. All the same, the bubble of recklessness that had been simmering within her since she'd followed Francesco off the dance floor the night before grew within her.

It was her turn to bet. Both she and her opponent had already put a large wedge of chips into the pot.

Where was Francesco? He'd said he would be there socialising with the guests.

He wasn't in the room, but somehow she just *knew* he was watching her.

Her heart hammering, she pushed her remaining chips forward. *Please* let Francesco be watching. 'All in.'

Her opponent stared at her, a twitch forming under his left eye.

She stared back, giving nothing away.

He rubbed his chin.

She knew before he did that he was going to fold, hid her feelings of triumph that she'd successfully bluffed him.

The big pile of poker chips was hers.

It would appear that her long-practised poker face had become a blessing in itself.

Francesco could hardly believe what he was witnessing over the monitors.

Hannah was a card shark. There was no other way to describe the way she played, which, if you were in a position to see the cards she'd been dealt, as he was, at times verged on the reckless. Not that her opponents could see how recklessly she played. All they saw was the cool facade, the face that didn't give away a single hint of emotion.

For a woman who had never played the game before, it was masterful. And yet...

Something deep inside his gut clenched when he considered why she'd been able to develop such a good poker face. Only someone who'd spent years hiding their emotions could produce it so naturally. He should know. He'd been perfecting his own version for years.

When she'd knocked her fourth opponent out... The way she'd pushed her chips forward, the clear *simpatico* way she'd said, 'All in...'

His gut had tightened further. Somehow he'd known those two little words meant more than just the chips before her.

It didn't take long before she'd demolished her final opponent. Only when she'd won that final hand did that beautiful smile finally break on her face, a smile of genuine delight that had all her defeated opponents reaching over to shake her hand and kiss her cheeks. The mostly male crowd surrounding her also muscled in, finding it necessary to embrace her when giving their congratulations.

They wouldn't look twice if they could see her in her usual state, Francesco thought narkily. They would be so blinkered they would never see her for the natural beauty she was.

'I'm going back down,' he said, heading to the reinforced steel door. For some reason, his good mood, induced by dinner with Hannah, had plummeted.

Striding across the main playing area of the third floor, he ignored all attempts from players and staff to meet his eyes.

With play in the tournament temporarily halted so the players who'd made it through to the second round could take a break, he found Hannah sipping coffee, surrounded by a horde of men all impressing their witticisms and manliness upon her.

When she saw him, her eyes lit up, then dimmed as she neared him.

'What's the matter?' she asked.

'Nothing.'

'Ooh, you liar. You look like someone's stolen your granny's false teeth and you've been told to donate your own as a replacement.'

Her good humour had zero effect on his blackening mood. 'And you look like you're having fun,' he said pointedly, unable to contain the ice in his voice.

'Isn't that the whole point of me entering the tournament? Didn't you tell me to enjoy myself?'

Francesco took a deep breath, Hannah's bewilderment

reminding him he had no good reason to be acting like a jealous fool.

Jealousy?

Was that really what the strong compulsion running through him to throw her over his shoulder and carry her out of the casino and away from all these admiring men was?

His father, for all his catting about with other women half his age, had been consumed with it. His mother had suffered more than one beating at his hands for daring to look at another man the wrong way.

Francesco had assumed that, in his own case, jealousy had skipped a generation. The closest he'd come to that particular emotion had been in his early twenties. Then, he'd learned Luisa, a girl he was seeing, was two-timing him with Pepe Mastrangelo, whom she'd sworn she'd finished with. That hadn't been jealousy, though—that had been pure anger, a rage that had heightened when he learned she'd tricked him out of money so she could hightail it to the UK for an abortion. So duplicitous had she been, she'd no idea if he or Pepe was the father.

He'd despised Luisa for her lies, but not once had he wanted to seek Pepe out. Instead, Pepe had sought *him* out, his pain right there on the surface. But the only bruising Francesco had suffered had been to his ego, and the fight between them had been over before it started.

To learn he was as vulnerable to jealousy's clutches as the next man brought him up short, reminding him that he had Calvetti blood running inside him.

Salvatore Calvetti would never have walked away from the Luisa and Pepe debacle as Francesco had done. If Salvatore had walked in his shoes, Luisa would have been scarred for life. Pepe would likely have disappeared, never to be seen again.

But he didn't want to be anything like Salvatore.

He never wanted to treat *anyone* the way his father had treated his mother.

Raking his fingers through his hair, a growl escaped from his throat. Whether he liked it or not, Calvetti blood ran through his veins.

Just one more reason why he should never touch her.

Hannah looked as if she wanted to say something, but the gong sounded for the second round. She was placed on table one. Her chips were passed to her. Francesco watched as she stacked them into neat piles, oblivious to the crowd forming around her table.

The strength of his possessiveness had him clenching his fists. Was she really so ignorant of the admiring glances and lecherous stares?

She raised her eyes to meet his glare and gave a hesitant smile. He looked away.

A discreet cough behind him caught his attention. He turned to find his general manager standing there.

'We have the proof—the blackjack player *is* cheating us,' he said, his lips barely moving.

'Give me a few minutes.' Francesco barely bothered trying to hide his impatience.

Hannah was still looking at him, a puzzled groove in her forehead.

'I can get the ball moving…'

'I *said*, give me a few minutes.' The blackjack cheat could wait. Francesco would not step a foot away from the room until Hannah was done with the tournament. His presence was the only thing stopping the fawning men from trying their luck that bit harder.

She was done much earlier than he'd envisaged. From playing the first round like a pro and with a good dollop of luck, her game fell to pieces and she was the first player out.

She shrugged, smiled gracefully, took a sip of water, and leaned back in her chair.

He was by her side in seconds. 'Come, it is time for us to move elsewhere,' he said, speaking into her ear, ignoring the curious stares of all those surrounding them.

'I want to watch the rest of the tournament.'

'You can watch it from my security office. There are things I need to attend to.'

Hannah turned to face him. 'Go and attend to them, then,' she said with a shrug.

'But I require your company.' Or, rather, he wanted to get her away from this room full of letches.

Swivelling her chair around with exceptionally bad grace, she got to her feet.

'What is the matter with you?' he asked as they swept through the room and out of the door.

'Me?' Incredulous, Hannah stopped walking and placed a hand on her hip. 'I was having a lovely time until you came in looking as if you wanted to kill me.' Seriously, how could anyone concentrate with Francesco's handsome face glowering at them? 'You totally put me off my game, and then you dragged me out before I could enjoy watching the rest of it.'

She glared at him. She'd had such a wonderful meal, had thought he'd enjoyed himself, too, the aloof, arrogant man unbending into something infinitely more human that warmed her from the inside out. But now he'd reverted, and was more aloof and arrogant than ever.

'It wasn't you that angered me.'

She folded her arms and raised a brow in a perfect imitation of him. 'Really?'

'Did you not see the way those men were looking at you? As if you were a piece of meat.'

'They were just being friendly.' Men *never* looked at her

MICHELLE SMART   99

in that way. Not that she ever met men outside the hospital environment, she conceded.

'Take a look in the mirror, Dr Chapman. You're a beautiful woman.'

His unexpected compliment let loose a cluster of fluttering butterflies in her belly.

'And I'm sorry for putting you off your game—you're quite a player.'

'You think?' His compliment—for it was definitely a compliment coming from him—warmed her insides even further, making her forget to be cross with him.

He smiled, an honest-to-goodness smile, and reached out to touch a loose tendril of her hair. 'If you were to give up medicine, you could make a good living on the poker circuit.'

The butterflies in her belly exploded. Heat surged through her veins, her insides liquefying.

Was it her imagination, or was the longing she could feel swirling inside her mirrored in his eyes...?

Dropping his hand from her hair, he traced a finger down her cheek.

She shivered, her skin heating beneath his touch.

'Come. I need to attend to business,' he said before steering her off to the top floor, not quite touching her but keeping her close enough that she was constantly aware of his heat, of *him*.

'What are we going up here for?' she asked once she'd managed to get her tongue working again. But, oh, it was so hard to think straight when the skin on her cheek still tingled from his touch.

'A player from the second-floor has been caught cheating. Stealing from us.'

'Have you called the police?'

He looked at her as if she'd asked if the moon was made of chocolate. 'That is not how we do things here.'

'How do you do things…?' The strangest look flitted over her face. 'Oh. You break hands.'

The sadness in Hannah's tone cut through him. Francesco paused to look at her properly. 'The punishment is determined by the crime.'

'But surely if a crime has been committed then the police should be left to deal with it? That's what they're paid for after all.'

'This is Sicily, Dr Chapman. The rules are different here.'

'Because that's what you were taught by your father?'

Her question caught him up short. 'It's nothing to do with my father. It's about respect and following the rules.'

'But who makes the rules? This is *your* empire, Francesco. Your father isn't here anymore. You're an adult. Your actions are your own.'

The air caught in his lungs, an acrid taste forming in his throat. 'Do you have an answer for everything?'

'Not even close.' She looked away, avoiding his gaze. 'If it's all the same to you, I'd like to wait downstairs.' Her tone had become distant.

His stomach rolled over. 'Nothing will happen to the cheating thief on these premises.'

'I don't want anything to happen to him off the premises, either. I'm a doctor, Francesco. I can't be—won't be—a party to anything that harms another person. I know this is your life and what you're used to, but for me…' She shook her head. 'I could never live with myself. Can you get one of your men to take me back to the villa?'

'Wait in the bar for me,' he said. 'I'll be with you in ten minutes.'

Not smiling, she nodded her acquiescence and walked

back down the stairs, gripping onto the gold handrail as she made her descent.

Francesco's chest felt weighted, although he knew not why.

He never made any apologies for his life and the way his world worked. Hannah knew the score—he'd never hidden anything from her. He'd *told* her what it was like. He'd warned her. In fact, it was the only reason he'd brought her here, so she could see for herself that he was not worth wasting her virginity on. It was not his fault she hadn't listened.

So why was the only thing he could see as he pushed the door open the sad disappointment dulling her eyes?

He entered the manager's office. Mario and Roberto, another of his most trusted men, were already there, along with the cheat.

Up close, he could see the cheat was a young man in his early twenties, who looked as if he should be playing computer games with an online community of other awkward young men, not systematically ripping off casinos across the Continent. He sat in the middle of the room. He looked terrified.

There was a tap on the door and the manager walked in, handing Francesco a dossier on the blackjack player's activity. It made for quick reading.

Mario watched him, waiting for the nod.

This was the part of the job Francesco liked the least. When he'd first bought into this, his first casino, three years ago, he'd employed his father's old henchmen, knowing them to be reliable and loyal. Within months, he'd paid the majority of them off when it became clear they expected to continue using the methods enjoyed by Salvatore as punishment. While he had always respected his father, Francesco had always known that when the time came for him to take over, his methods would be different, less extreme.

Mario was Francesco's man and capable of great restraint. Apart from one drug dealer who'd frequented Francesco's Naples nightclub and who they'd discovered was pimping out vulnerable teenage girls, he never made the punishments personal and never caused damage that would not heal.

When he gave the nod, Mario and Roberto would take the young man somewhere private. They would teach him a lesson he would never forget—a lesson that rarely needed to be given, as most people were not stupid enough to try to cheat a Calvetti casino. Francesco's reputation preceded him. And, really, this was the perfect opportunity to rid himself of Hannah. It was clear this whole situation had unsettled her enough to at least consider getting a flight home. If he gave the nod, he could guarantee she would be on the first flight back to England....

Yet her insinuation that he was following in his father's brutish footsteps jabbed him like a spear.

He was *not* his father. If this young cheat had tried any such behaviour in any of Salvatore's businesses, he would have disappeared. For ever.

Rules were rules, even if they were only unwritten. They were there for a reason.

His father would never have dreamed of breaking them....

Hannah nursed her strong coffee, gazing absently at the huge flat-screen television against a wall of the bar showing music videos. She didn't want to think of what was happening on the floor above her. If she thought about it hard enough she might just scream.

But when she tried not to think about it, thoughts of Melanie's wedding filled the space instead.

How could she endure it? Every morning she woke knowing the nuptials were one day closer, the knot in her belly tightening another notch.

She would give anything to get out of going, but even if an excuse came fully presented on a plate she would not be able to take it. Melanie had appointed her maid of honour, a role Hannah knew she did not deserve.

The wedding was something she would have to find a way to cope with. Whatever it took, she would try to keep smiling so her little sister could walk down the aisle without her day being ruined.

'Due bicchieri di champagne.'

Francesco's sudden appearance at her side startled her.

'Hi,' she said dully, hating that her heart thumped just to see him.

'Ciao.' He nodded. 'I've just ordered us each a glass of champagne.'

'You said you would take me back to the villa.'

'And I will. Five minutes. You look as if you need a drink.'

'I need to get my phone and my passport, and go home. To England,' she added in case her meaning wasn't absolutely clear.

Francesco had been right from the start. She really didn't belong in his world, not even on a temporary basis.

The injuries to Mario had been inflicted a long time ago and were, in effect, history. Mario's loyalty to Francesco only served to reinforce this notion of a long-forgotten event, something that had no bearing on the present.

The person they'd caught stealing tonight... This was now; this *was* the present.

Hannah was a doctor. She had dedicated her life to

saving lives. She could never be a party to someone else's injury.

'Come, Dr Chapman. You are supposed to be living a little. You are here to see something of the world and experience the things that have passed you by. You hardly touched your wine at dinner.'

'I'm really not in the mood.'

Pressing his lips to her ear, he said, 'I called the police.'

Her head whipped round so quickly she almost butted his nose. 'Seriously?'

Two glasses of champagne were placed before them. Francesco picked them up and nodded at a corner sofa. Thoroughly confused, she followed him.

Sitting gingerly next to him, she would have ignored the champagne had he not thrust it into her hand.

'Drink. You need to relax a little—you're far too tense.'

'Did you really call the police?'

'As you implied, I make the rules.' A slight smile played on his lips. 'I thought about the prison system here. When I said I was calling the police, the thief begged for a beating.'

She couldn't contain the smile that spread over her face or the hand that rose to palm his cheek. 'See? I *was* right about you.'

At his quizzical expression, she added, 'I knew there was good within you. You proved it by taking care of me so well after my accident, and now you've reaffirmed it.'

He shook his head. 'It's just for this one time, okay? And only because I respect your profession and the oath you took.'

'If you say so.' A feeling of serenity swept through her. Stroking her fingers down his cheek, she took a sip of her champagne.

'Better?'

She nodded. 'Much. I'll feel even better when I have my phone back.' She felt lost without it.

'Finish your champagne and I will take you back.'

His eyes bored into her, *daring* her to drink it. The sip she'd had still danced on her tongue, tantalising her, just as Francesco tantalised her.

This was why she was here, she reminded herself. Not to involve herself in the intricacies of his life but to experience her *own*.

Putting the flute back to her lips, she tipped the sparkling liquid into her mouth and drank it in three swallows.

A grin spread across his face, somehow making him even more handsome, a feat she hadn't thought possible.

'Good for you.' He downed his own glass before rising to his feet. 'Come. It is time to take you back.'

Hannah grabbed her clutch bag and stood. Her body felt incredibly light.

Surrounded by Francesco's minders, who'd been waiting in the corner of the bar for them, they left. When they reached the stairs, he placed a hand on the small of her back, a protective gesture that lightened her even further.

CHAPTER EIGHT

FRANCESCO'S VILLA WAS in darkness, but as soon as his driver brought the car over the foot of the driveway, light illuminated it, bathing it in a golden hue. With the stars in the moonless night sky twinkling, it was the prettiest sight Hannah had ever seen.

'Can I get you a drink?' Francesco asked once they were alone inside, his minders having left for their own quarters. 'How about a brandy?'

The effects of the champagne had started to abate a little, but did she want to risk putting any more alcohol into her system?

'Only a small one,' he added, clearly reading her mind.

'Yes, please. A small one,' she agreed, hugging herself.

She followed him through the sprawling reception and into the living room, where Francesco swept a small white object from the windowsill. 'Catch,' he said, throwing it at her.

Luckily she caught it. Before she could admonish him for the reckless endangerment of her phone, he'd continued through the huge library, through the dining room, diverted round the indoor swimming pool, stepped through huge French doors and out onto a veranda overhanging the outdoor pool.

It was like stepping into a tropical-party area where the

only thing missing was the guests. A bar—a proper bar, with flashing lights, high stools, and everything—was set up at one end. Tables, chairs, and plump sofas abounded.

'I bet you have some fantastic parties here,' she said. The perfect setting for the playboy Francesco was reputed to be, yet, she reflected, not at all the man who she was learning he was.

'Not for a long time.'

'Why's that?'

'I have different priorities now.' He raised his shoulder, affecting nonchalance, but there was no doubting the 'I'm not prepared to discuss this' timbre in his voice.

That was fine by her. She doubted she wanted to know what his new priorities were anyway.

She spotted a long white board jutting through the trellis. 'Is that a diving board?'

He nodded. 'It beats walking down the steps to reach the swimming pool.'

'You should get a slide—that would be much more fun.'

He chuckled and slipped behind the bar. 'That's not a bad idea. Do you swim?'

'Not for years.'

'I would suggest a dip now but alcohol and swimming pools do not mix well. We will have time for a swim in the morning—that is, if you want to stay the night. Or do you still want to get a flight home?'

There was no mistaking the meaning in his quietly delivered words.

A thrill of excitement speared up her spine, making her shiver despite the warmth of her skin in the balmy night air.

Dimly she recalled saying she wanted to go home. The anger that had made her say those words had gone. All that lay within her now was a longing, wrapped so tightly in her chest it almost made her nauseous.

This was what she'd wanted. It was the whole reason she was here.

She shook her head. 'I don't want to go home. I want to stay.'

His eyes held hers, heat flashing from them before he reached for a bottle and poured them both a drink, topping the smaller measure with a splash of lemonade. He handed it to her. 'I've sweetened it for you, otherwise your untried taste buds might find it a little too harsh.'

Their fingers brushed as she took the glass from him. That same flash of heat sparked in his eyes again.

'*Saluti*,' he said, holding his glass aloft.

'*Saluti*,' she echoed, chinking her glass to his.

Francesco took a swallow of his drink. 'I thought you would have checked your phone by now.'

'Oh.' Disconcerted, she blinked. 'I should, really.' After all the fuss she'd made over it, she'd shoved it into her clutch bag without even checking the screen for messages.

For the first time since she'd gained her permanent place on the children's ward, the compulsion to check her phone had taken second place to something else. And that something else was gazing at Francesco.

The more she looked at him, the more the excited nausea increased. Was it even nausea she felt? She didn't know; she had no name befitting the ache that pulsed so, so low within her.

While she stood there rooted, helpless for the first time to know what to do, all her bravado and certainty from the night before gone, Francesco finished his brandy and laid the glass on the bar. 'Time for bed.'

Bed...

Immediately the butterflies inside her began to thrash about, her heart racing at a gallop.

It was late. She'd been awake the best part of two days

after a night of hardly any sleep, yet she didn't feel the least bit weary.

But sleep wasn't what Francesco was implying with his statement.

She gulped her drink down, completely forgetting it had alcohol in it. It had a bitter aftertaste that somehow soothed her skittering nerves a touch. She felt like grabbing the bottle and pouring herself another, this time without the lemonade.

Francesco must have read what was going on beneath her skin, for he stepped out from behind the bar and stood before her. He reached out a hand and pulled her chopsticks out. After a moment's suspended animation her hair tumbled down.

'That's better,' he murmured. Before she could ask what he meant, he inhaled deeply and took a step back. 'I'm going to my room. I will let you decide if you want to join me in it or if you wish to sleep alone.'

'But...'

'I can see you're nervous. I want you to be sure. I meant what I said last night—I will not take advantage of you. My room is two doors from yours. I leave the ball in your court.' With that, he bowed his head, turned on his heel, and strode away.

After a long pause in which all the blood in her body flooded into her brain and roared around her ears, Hannah expelled a long breath of air.

What had she expected? That Francesco would take charge, sweep her into his arms, and carry her manfully all the way to his bedroom as if she weighed little more than a bag of sugar? That he would lay her on his bed and devour her, taking command of every touch and movement?

Hadn't she known he was far too honourable for that?

How right she had been that he would never do anything

to hurt her—even taking her phone had been, according to Francesco's sense of logic, for her own good. Saying that, if he ever stole it from her again she certainly wouldn't be so forgiving.... Oh, what was she thinking? After tonight he would never have another opportunity to steal her phone. Once this weekend was over she would throw herself back into her work—her life—and Francesco would be nothing but a memory of one weekend when she'd dared embrace life in its entirety.

If she wanted Francesco to make love to her, she would have to go to him....

But could she do that? Could she slip into his room and slide under his bedcovers?

Could she not?

No. She couldn't *not* do it.

She would never meet another man like him—how could she when she'd spent twenty-seven years having never met *anyone* who made her feel anything?

It had all felt so different last night, though, when she'd practically begged him to make love to her. Before she'd spent time with him and discovered the complex man behind the cool facade, the man who could be both cruel and yet full of empathy. A man who was capable of both great brutality and great generosity. He was no longer some mythological dream figure. He was flesh and blood, with all the complexity that came from being human.

Francesco stood under the shower for an age, fixing the temperature to a much lower setting than the steaming-hot he usually favoured. If he kept it cold enough it might just do something to lessen his libido.

He pressed his forehead to the cool tiles.

Hannah was his for the taking. She'd been his for the taking since she'd first strolled into his nightclub carrying a bunch of flowers for him. All he had to do was walk two doors down and she would welcome him into her arms.

It unnerved him how badly he wanted to do that. How badly he wanted her.

Would she come to him?

He honestly could not guess.

She was not one of the worldly women he normally spent time with, for whom sex was a form of currency.

Hannah was a twenty-seven-year-old virgin who'd hidden the essence of herself from the world—from herself, even—for the best part of fifteen years.

He'd seen the hesitation in her eyes when he'd said it was time for bed. All the boldness from the night before had vanished, leaving her vulnerability lying right there on the surface.

He would not be the man to take advantage of that vulnerability, no matter how easy it would be and no matter how much she would welcome it.

Francesco could pinpoint the exact moment when the determination to keep her out of his bed had shifted. It had been when he'd looked at that cheating thief, a man so like all those other men who'd been fawning over her during the poker tournament. Now that Hannah's sexuality had awoken, it wouldn't meekly lie back down when she returned to London and return to its former dormancy. Eventually she would meet another man she wanted enough to make love to. It could be any of those men. It could be any man, not one of whom could be trusted to treat her with the tenderness she deserved.

Hannah wanted *him*.

And, *caro Dio*, he wanted her, too, with a need that burned in the very fabric of his being.

But he knew that this final step had to come from her

and her alone, however agonising the wait for her decision would be.

Stepping out of the shower, he towelled himself dry, brushed his teeth, and wandered naked through the doorway of the en suite bathroom into his bedroom....

While he'd showered, Hannah had crept into his room. She stood before the window, her eyes widening as she took in his nude form.

'You've taken your make-up off,' he said, walking slowly towards her. She'd showered, too, her hair damp, her body wrapped in the thick white bathrobe kept in the guest room.

She raised a hand to a cheek, which, even in the dim light, he could see had flushed with colour.

He covered her hand with his own. 'This is better. You're beautiful as you are.'

She trembled, although whether that was down to the hoarseness of his voice or a reaction to his touch he could not say.

Slowly he trailed a hand down the swan of her neck to the V made by the bathrobe, slipping a finger between the bunched material to loosen it, exposing the cleavage of her creamy breasts. Slower still, he slid down to the sash and, using both hands, untied it before pushing the robe apart, exposing her to him.

Hannah's breaths became shallow. Her chest hitched. She stood as still as a statue, staring at him with a look that somehow managed to be both bold and shy. He pushed the shoulders of the robe so it fell softly to the floor.

His own breath hitched as he drank her in.

Her body was everything he'd imagined and more—her breasts fuller and higher, her belly softly toned, her hips curvier, her legs longer and smoother.

He swallowed, the ache in his groin so deep it was painful.

He forced himself to remember that she was a virgin. No matter how badly he wanted to go ahead and devour her, he needed to keep the reins on himself.

Hannah had never felt so exposed—had never *been* so exposed—as she was at that moment. Her heart thundered, her blood surged, but none of it mattered. The hunger in Francesco's eyes was enough to evaporate the shyness and quell any last-minute fears, although, when she dared cast her eyes down to his jutting erection, she experienced a different, more primitive fear that was accompanied by a wild surge of heat through her loins.

Naked except for the gold cross that rested at the top of his muscular chest, Francesco was truly glorious. For such a tall, powerful man he had a surprising grace about him, an elegance to his raw masculinity that tempered the powerhouse he was.

Moisture filled her mouth. She swallowed it away, her eyes captured by the heat of hot chocolate fudge that gleamed.

She wanted to touch him. She wanted to rake her fingers through the whorls of dark hair covering his chest, to feel his skin beneath her lips.

Except she was rooted to the spot on which she stood, helpless to do anything but receive his study of her naked form.

'We'll take it very slowly,' he said, his words thick.

She couldn't speak, could only jerk a nod, aching for it to start, yearning for it to be over, a whole jumble of thoughts and emotions careering through her. Out of the fear and excitement, though, it was the latter that rose to the top.

This was it....

And then she was aloft, clutched against Francesco's hard torso as he swept her into his arms and carried her over to the enormous four-poster bed, her private fantasy coming to life.

Gently he laid her down on her back before lying beside her. He placed a hand on her collarbone—the same bone that had been broken during the moment that had brought him into her life—before slanting his lips on hers.

The heat from his mouth, the mintiness of his breath, the fresh oaky scent of him…sent her senses reeling. His kiss was light but assured, a tender pressure that slowly deepened until her lips parted and his tongue swept into her mouth.

Finally she touched him, placing a hand on his shoulder, feeling the smoothness of his skin while she revelled in the headiness evoked by his increasingly hungry kisses.

He moved his mouth away, sweeping his lips over her cheek to nibble at her earlobe. 'Are you sure about this?'

'You have to ask?' In response to the low resonance of his voice, her own was a breathless rush.

'Any time you want to stop, say.'

She turned her head to capture his lips. 'I don't want to stop.'

He groaned and muttered something she didn't understand before kissing her with such passion her bones seemed to melt within her.

His large hand swept over her, flattening against her breasts, trailing over her belly, stroking her, moulding her. And then he followed it with his mouth. When his lips closed over a puckered nipple she gasped, her eyes flying open.

Always she had looked at breasts as functional assets, understanding in a basic fashion that men lusted after them. Never had it occurred to her that the pleasure a man took from them could be reciprocated by the woman—by *her*. She reached for him, digging her fingers into his scalp, silently begging him to carry on, almost crying out when he broke away, only to immediately turn his attention to the other.

It was the most wonderful feeling imaginable.

At some point he had rolled on top of her. She could feel his erection prod against her thigh and moaned as she imagined what it would feel like to actually have him inside her, being a part of her...

Oh, but she burned, a delicious heat that seeped into every inch of her being, every part alive and dancing in the flames.

It was as if Francesco was determined to kiss and worship every tiny crevice, his mouth now trailing down over her belly whilst his hands...

Her gasp was loud when he moved a hand between her legs, gently stroking his fingers over her soft hair until he found her—

Dear God...

He knelt between her legs, his tongue *there*, pressed against her tight bud.

What was happening to her?

Never in her wildest imaginings had she dreamed that the very essence of her being could ache with such intensity. Nothing. Nothing could have prepared her.

Oh, but this was incredible—*he* was incredible...

Right in her core the heaviness grew. Francesco stayed exactly where he was, his tongue making tiny circular motions, increasing the pressure until, with a cry that seemed to come from a faraway land, ripples of pure pleasure exploded through her and carried her off to that faraway land in the stars.

Only when all the pulsations had abated did Francesco move, trailing kisses all the way back up her body until he reached her mouth and kissed her with a savagery that stole her remaining breath.

He lifted his head to gaze down at her. The chocolate in his eyes had fully melted, his expression one of wonder. 'I need to get some protection,' he said, sounding pained.

She didn't want him to leave her. She wanted him to stay right there, to keep her body covered with the heat of his own.

He didn't go far, simply rolling off her to reach into his bedside table. Before he could rip the square foil open, she placed her hand on his chest. Francesco's heart thudded as wildly as her own.

Closing her eyes, she twisted onto her side and pressed a kiss to his shoulder. And another. And another, breathing in his musky scent, rubbing her nose against the smoothness of his olive skin.

With trembling fingers she explored him, the hard chest with the soft black hair, the brown nipples that she rubbed a thumb over and heard him catch a breath at, the washboard stomach covered with a fine layer of that same black hair that thickened the lower she went, becoming more wiry...

She hesitated, raising her head from his shoulder to stare at him. How she longed to touch him properly, but there was a painful awareness that she didn't know what she was doing. How could she know what he liked, how he wanted to be touched? It wasn't that she had minimal experience—she had *no* experience. Nothing.

'You can do whatever you want,' he whispered hoarsely, raking his hands through her hair and pressing a kiss to her lips. 'Touch me however you like.'

Could he read her mind?

Tentatively, she encircled her hand around his length, feeling it pulsate beneath her touch. Francesco groaned and lay back, hooking one arm over his head while the other lay buried in her hair, his fingers massaging her scalp.

His erection felt a lot smoother than she'd expected, and as she moved her hand up to the tip, a drop of fluid rubbed in her fingers.

A rush of moist heat flooded between her legs, a sharp pulsation, the same ache she had experienced when Francesco had set her body alight with his mouth. To witness his desire for her was as great an aphrodisiac as anything she had experienced since being in his room.

So quickly she didn't even notice him move, he covered her hand with his. 'No more,' he growled. 'I want to be inside you.'

She couldn't resist wrapping an arm around his neck and kissing him, pressing herself against him as tightly as she could.

Hooking an arm around her waist, Francesco twisted her back down, sliding a knee between her legs to part them.

With expert deftness, he ripped the foil open with his teeth and rolled it on before manoeuvring himself so he was fully on top of her and between her parted thighs, his erection heavy against her.

He pressed his lips to hers and kissed her, his left hand burying back into her hair, his right sliding down her side and slipping between them.

She felt him guide the tip of his erection against her and then into her, and sucked in a breath. Francesco simply deepened the kiss, murmuring words of Sicilian endearment into her mouth. He brought his hand back up to stroke her face and thrust forward a little more, still kissing her, stroking her, nibbling at the sensitive skin of her neck, slowly, slowly inching his way inside her.

There was one moment of real discomfort that made her freeze, but then it was gone, her senses too full of Francesco and all the magical things he was doing to dwell on that one thing.

And then he was there, all the way inside her, stretching her, filling her massively, his groin pressed against her pubis, his chest crushing against her breasts.

'Am I hurting you?' he asked raggedly.

'No. It feels…good.' It felt more than good—it felt heavenly.

'*You* feel so good,' he groaned into her ear, withdrawing a little only to inch forward again.

His movements were slow but assured, allowing her to adjust to all these new feelings and sensations, building the tempo at an unhurried pace, only pulling back a few inches, keeping his groin pressing against her.

The sensations he'd created with his tongue began to bubble within her again but this time felt fuller, deeper, more condensed.

Her arms wrapped around his neck, her breaths shallow, she began to move with him, meeting his thrusts, which steadily lengthened. And all the while he kissed her, his hands roaming over the sides of her body, her face, her neck, her hair…everywhere.

She felt the tension increase within him, his groans deepening—such an erotic sound, confirmation that everything she was experiencing was shared, that it was real and not just a beautiful dream. The bubbling deep in her core thickened and swelled, triggering a mass of pulsations to ripple through her. Crying out, she clung to him, burying her face in his neck at the same moment Francesco gave his own cry and made one final thrust that seemed to last for ever.

CHAPTER NINE

FRANCESCO STRETCHED, LOOKED at his bedside clock, then turned back over to face the wall that was Hannah's back. When they'd fallen into sleep she'd been cuddled into him, their limbs entwined.

The last time he'd had such a deep sleep had been his birthday ten months ago. That had been just two days before he'd discovered his mother's diaries.

For the first time in ten months he'd fallen asleep without the demons that plagued him screwing with his thoughts.

Only the top of Hannah's shoulder blades were uncovered and he resisted the urge to place a kiss on them. After disposing of the condom, he'd longed to make love to her again. He'd put his selfish desires to one side. She'd had a long week at work, little sleep the night before, and her body was bound to ache after making love for the first time. Instead he'd pulled her to him and listened to her fall into slumber. It was the sweetest sound he'd ever heard.

He rubbed his eyes and pinched the bridge of his nose, expelling a long breath.

If someone had told him just twenty-four hours ago that making love to Hannah Chapman would be the best experience of his life, he would have laughed. And not with any humour.

To know he was the first man to have slept with her

made his chest fill. To know that he'd awoken those responses… It had been a revelation, a thing of beauty.

Francesco had never felt humble about anything in his life, yet it was the closest he could come to explaining the gratitude he felt towards her for choosing him.

Hannah hadn't chosen him for his power or his wealth or his lifestyle—she'd chosen and trusted him for *him*.

To think he'd dismissed her when she'd blurted out that she wanted him to make love to her. She could have accepted that dismissal. Eventually she would have found another man she trusted enough…

It didn't bear thinking about.

The thought of another man pawing at her and making clumsy love to her made his brain burn and his heart clench.

Suddenly he became aware that her deep, rhythmic breathing had stopped.

His suspicion that she'd awoken was confirmed when she abruptly turned over to face him, her eyes startled.

'*Buongiorno,*' he said, a smile already playing on his lips.

Blinking rapidly, Hannah covered a yawn before bestowing him with a sleepy smile. 'What time is it?'

'Nine o'clock.'

She yawned again. 'Wow. I haven't slept in that late for years.'

'You needed it.' Hooking an arm around her waist, he pulled her to him. 'How are you feeling?'

Her face scrunched in thought. 'Strange.'

'Good strange or bad strange?'

That wonderful look of serenity flitted over her face. 'Good strange.'

Already his body ached to make love to her again. Trailing his fingers over her shoulder, enjoying the softness of her skin, he pressed a kiss to her neck. 'Are you hungry?'

His lust levels rose when she whispered huskily into his ear, 'Starving.'

A late breakfast was brought out to them on the bar-side veranda. Their glasses from the previous evening had already been cleared away.

Wrapped in the guest robe, her hair damp from the shower she'd shared with Francesco, Hannah stretched her legs out and took a sip of the deliciously strong yet sweet coffee. Sitting next to her, dressed in his own dark grey robe, his thigh resting against hers, Francesco grinned.

'You are so lucky waking up to this view every morning,' she sighed. With the morning sun rising above them, calm waves swirling onto Francesco's private beach in the distance, it was as if they were in their own private nirvana.

Breakfast usually consisted of a snatched slice of toast. Today she'd been treated to eggs and bacon and enough fresh rolls and fruit to feed a whole ward of patients.

Yes. Nirvana.

'Believe me, this is the best view I've had in a *very* long time,' he said, his eyes gleaming, his deep voice laced with meaning.

Thinking of all the beautiful women she'd seen pictured on his arm, Hannah found that extremely hard to believe.

Her belly twisted.

It was no good thinking of all those women. Comparing herself to them would be akin to comparing a rock to the moon.

For the first time in her life she wished she'd put some make-up on, then immediately scolded herself for such a ridiculous thought. All those women who had the time and inclination to doll themselves up…well, good luck to them. Even after the make-up lesson she'd been given in the salon, painting her face for their night out had felt like wasted time. Looking at her reflection once she was done had been like looking at a stranger. She hadn't felt like *her*.

She supposed she could always look at it as practice for Melanie's wedding, though—a thought that brought a lump to her throat.

'You do realise you're the sexiest woman on the planet, don't you?' Francesco's words broke through the melancholy of her thoughts.

'Hardly,' she spluttered, taking another sip of her coffee.

'I can prove it,' he murmured sensually into her ear, clasping her hand and tugging it down to rest on his thigh. Sliding it up to his groin, he whispered, 'You see, my clever doctor, you are irresistible.' As he spoke, he nibbled into the nape of her neck, keeping a firm grip on her hand, moving it up so she could feel exactly what effect she was having on him.

A thrill of heady power rushed through her. Heat pooled between her legs, her breath deserting her.

They'd already made love twice since she'd awoken. She'd thought she was spent, had assumed Francesco was, too.

With his free hand he tugged her robe open enough to slip a hand through and cup a breast, kneading it gently. 'You also have the most beautiful breasts on the earth,' he murmured into her ear before sliding his lips over to her mouth and kissing her with a ferocity that reignited the remaining embers of her desire.

'What…what if one of your staff comes out?' she gasped, moving him with more assurance as he unclasped her hand and snaked his arm round her waist,

'They won't.' Thus saying, he slid his hand under her bottom and lifted her off the chair and onto the table, ignoring the fact that their breakfast plates and cups were scattered all over it.

Francesco ached to be inside her again, his body fired up beyond belief, and such a short time after their last bout. It was those memories of being in the shower with her, when she'd sunk to her knees and taken him in her mouth for the first time....

Just thinking about it would sustain his fantasies for a lifetime.

Dipping his head to take a perfectly ripe breast into his mouth, he trailed a hand down her belly and slipped a finger inside her, groaning aloud to find her hot and moist and ready for him.

Diving impatiently into his pocket, he grabbed the condom he'd put in there as an afterthought and, with Hannah distracting him by smothering any part of his face and neck she could reach with kisses, he slipped it on, spread her thighs wide, and plunged straight into her tight heat.

Her head lolled back, her eyes widening as if in shock.

Silently he cursed himself. Such was his excitement he'd totally forgotten that until a few short hours ago she'd been a virgin.

'Too much?' he asked, stilling, fighting to keep himself in check.

'Oh, no.' As if to prove it, she grabbed his buttocks and ground herself against him. The shock left her eyes, replaced with the desire he knew swirled in his own. 'I want it all.'

It was all he needed. Sweeping the crockery this way and that to make some space, he pushed her back so she was flat on the table, her thighs parted and raised high, her legs wrapped around his, and thrust into her, withdrawing to the tip and thrusting back in, over and over until she was whimpering beneath him, her hands flailing to grab his chest, her head turning from side to side. Only when he felt her thicken around him and her muscles contract did he let himself go, plunging in as deep as he could with one final groan before collapsing on top of her.

It was only when all the stars had cleared that he realised they were still in their respective robes, Hannah's fingers playing under the Egyptian cotton, tracing up and down his back.

She giggled.

Lifting his chin to rest it on her chest, he stared at her intently.

'That was incredible,' she said, smiling.

He flashed his teeth in return. 'You, *signorina*, are a very quick learner.'

'And you, *signor*, are a very good teacher.'

'There is so much more I can teach you.'

'And is it all depraved?'

'Most of it.'

She laughed softly and lay back on the table, expelling a sigh of contentment as she gazed up at the cobalt sky. He kept his gaze on her face. That serene look was there again. To think he was the cause of it...

A late breakfast turned into a late lunch. Francesco did not think he had ever felt the beat of the sun so strongly on his skin. For the first time in ten months he enjoyed a lazy day—indeed, the thought of working never crossed his mind. The rage he felt for his father, the rage that had boiled within him for so long, had morphed into a mild simmer.

In the back of his mind was the knowledge that at some point soon he would have to arrange for his jet to take Hannah back to London, but it was something he desisted from thinking about too much, content to make love, skinny-dip, then make love again. And she seemed happy, too, her smile serene, radiant.

Kissing her for what could easily be the thousandth time, he tied his robe around his waist and headed back indoors and to his bedroom for more condoms.

The box was almost empty. He shook his head in wonder. He'd never known desire like it. He couldn't get enough of her.

When he returned outside, Hannah had poured them both another cup of coffee from the pot and was curled up on one of the sofas reading something on her phone.

'Everything okay?' he asked, hiding the burst of irritation that poked at him.

This was the third time she'd gone through her messages since they'd awoken.

She's a dedicated professional, he reminded himself. Her patients are her priority, as they should be.

For all his sound reasoning, there was no getting around the fact he wanted to rip the phone from her hand and stamp on it. After all, it was the weekend. She was off duty.

She looked up and smiled. 'All's well.'

'Good.' Sitting next to her, he plucked the phone from her hand and slipped it into his pocket.

'Not again,' she groaned.

'Now you have satisfied yourself that your patients are all well, you have no need for it.'

'Francesco, give it back.'

'Later. You need to learn to switch off. Besides, it's rude.'

'Please.' Her voice lowered, all her former humour gone. 'That's my phone. And I wasn't being rude—you'd gone to the bedroom.' She held her hand out, palm side up. 'Now give.'

'What's it worth?' he asked, leaning into her, adopting a sensuous tone.

'Me not kicking you in the ankle.'

'I thought you didn't believe in violence.'

'So did I.' A smile suddenly creased her face and she burst out laughing, her mirth increasing when he shoved her phone back into the pocket of her robe. 'Now I get it—threats of violence really do work.'

He kissed her neck and flattened her onto her back. 'The difference is I knew you didn't mean it.'

Raking her fingers through his hair, she sighed. 'I guess you'll never know.'

'Oh, I know.' Hannah healed people. She didn't hurt them.

But he didn't want to think those thoughts. The time was fast approaching when he'd have to take her home, leaving him limited time left to worship her delectable body.

'I'm going to be in London more frequently for a while,' he mentioned casually, making his way down to a ripe breast. 'I'll give you a call when I'm over. Take you out for dinner.' With all the evidence pointing to Luca Mastrangelo still sniffing around the Mayfair casino, Francesco needed to be on the ball. If that meant spending more time in London, then so be it. The casino would be his, however he had to achieve it. He would secure that deal and nothing would prevent it.

Hannah moaned as he circled his tongue around a puckered nipple.

At least being in London more often meant he could enjoy her for a little longer, too.

It never occurred to him that Hannah might have different ideas.

Hannah opened the curtains and stepped into the cubicle, pulling the curtains shut around her. She smiled at the small girl lying in the bed who'd been brought in a week ago with encephalitis, inflammation of the brain, then smiled at the anxious parents. 'We have the lab results,' she said, not wasting time with pleasantries, 'and it's good news.'

This was her favourite part of the job, she thought a few minutes later as she walked back to her small workspace—telling parents who'd lived through hell that their child would make it, that the worst was over.

Clicking the mouse to get her desktop working, she opened the young girl's file, ready to write her notes up into the database. Her phone vibrated in her pocket.

She pulled it out, her heart skipping when Francesco's name flashed up.

Time seemed to still as she stared at it, her hands frozen.

Should she answer?

Or not?

It went to voicemail before she could decide.

Closing her eyes, she tilted her head back and rolled her neck.

Why, oh, why had she agreed to see him again? Not that she had agreed. At the time she'd been too busy writhing in his arms to think coherently about anything other than the sensations he was inducing in her....

She squeezed her eyes even tighter.

Francesco, in all his arrogance, had simply assumed she'd want to see him again.

An almost hysterical burst of laughter threatened to escape from her throat.

There was no way she could see him again. She just couldn't.

Their time together in Sicily had brought him, her dream man, to life—the good and the bad. Being with him had been the most wonderful, thrilling time imaginable. She had felt alive. She had felt *so much*.

She had felt *too much*.

All she wanted now was to focus on her job and leave Francesco as nothing but a beautiful memory.

She would carry on seeking out new experiences to share with Beth for when the time came that they were together again. But these experiences would be of an entirely different nature, more of a tick box—*I've done that, I've parachuted out of an aeroplane*—experience. Nothing that would clog her head. Nothing that would compromise everything she had spent the majority of her life working towards.

But, dear God, the hollowness that had lived in her chest for so long now felt so *full*, as if her shrivelled heart had been pumped back to life. And that scared her more than anything.

It was easier to shatter a full heart than a shrivelled one.

'Hannah, you should go home,' Alice, the ward sister said, startling her from her thoughts. Alice looked hard at her. 'Are you okay?'

Hannah nodded. Alice was lovely, a woman whose compassion extended from the children to all the staff on the ward. 'I'm fine,' she said, forcing a smile. 'I'll be off as soon as I get these reports finished.'

'It'll be dark soon,' Alice pointed out. 'Anyway, I'm off now. I'll see you in the morning.'

Alone again, Hannah rubbed her temples, willing away the tension headache that was forming.

She really should go home. Her shift had officially finished two hours ago.

The thought of returning to her little home filled her with nothing but dread, just as it had for the past three days since she'd returned from Sicily

Her home felt so empty.

The silence…how had she never noticed the silence before, when the only noise had been the sound of her own breathing?

For the first time ever, she felt lonely. Not the usual loneliness that had been within her since Beth's death, but a different kind of isolation. Colder, somehow.

Even the sunny yellow walls of her little cubbyhole felt bleak.

Francesco's phone rang. *'Ciao.'*

'That young drug dealer is back. We have him.'

'Bring him to me.'

Francesco knew exactly who Mario was on about. A young lad, barely eighteen, had visited his Palermo nightclub a few weeks ago. The cameras had caught him slipping bags of powder and pills to many of the clubbers. As unlikely as it was, he had slipped their net, escaping before Francesco's men could apprehend him, disappearing into the night.

He rubbed his eyes.

No matter how hard he tried to remove the dealers, there was always some other cocky upstart there to fill the breach. It was like trying to stop the tide.

The one good thing he could say about it was that at least he was making the effort to clean the place up, to counter some of the damage his father had done.

Salvatore had been responsible for channelling millions of euros' worth of drugs into Sicily and mainland Europe. How he had kept it secret from his son, Francesco would never understand; he could only guess Salvatore had known it was the one thing his son would never stand idly by and allow to happen. If Francesco *had* known, he would have ripped his father apart, but by the time he'd learned of his involvement, it had been too late to confront him. Salvatore had already been buried when he found out the truth.

It occurred to him, not for the first time, that his father had been afraid of him.

Slowly but surely, he was dismantling everything Salvatore Calvetti had built, closing it down brick by brick, taking care in his selection of which to dismantle first so as not to disturb the foundation and have it all crumble on top of him. Only a few days ago he had taken great delight in shutting down a restaurant that had been a hub for the distribution of arms, one of many in his father's great network.

While he'd been paying off Paolo di Luca, the man who'd run the restaurant on his father's behalf for thirty years, he had seen for the first time the old man Paolo had become. A man with liver spots and a rheumy wheeze. The more he thought about it, the more he realised all the old associates were exactly that—old.

When had they got so ancient?

These weren't the terrifying men of his childhood memories. Apart from a handful who hadn't taken kindly to being put out to pasture, most of them had been happy to be paid off, glad to spend their remaining years with their wives—or mistresses in many cases—and playing with their grandchildren and great-grandchildren.

There was a knock on the door, and the handle turned.

Mario and two of his other guards walked in, holding the young drug dealer up by the scruff of his neck.

With them came a burst of music from the club, a dreadful tune that hit him straight in his gut.

It was the same tune Hannah had been dancing to so badly in his London club, when he'd threatened the fool manhandling her.

The same Hannah who'd ignored her phone when he'd called and, in response to a message he'd sent saying he would be in London at the weekend, had sent him a simple message back saying she was busy. Since then…nothing. Not a peep from her.

It wasn't as if she never used her blasted phone. It was attached to her like an appendage.

There was no getting around it. She was avoiding him.

He looked at the belligerent drug dealer, but all he could see was the look of serenity on Hannah's face when he'd told her of calling the police on the casino cheat.

Hannah saved lives. She'd sworn an oath to never do harm.

What was it she'd said? *Who makes the rules?*

'Empty your pockets,' he ordered, not moving from his seat.

He could see how badly the drug dealer wanted to disobey him, but sanity prevailed and he emptied his pockets. He had two bags of what Francesco recognised as ecstasy tablets and a bag full of tiny cellophane wraps of white powder. Cocaine.

A cross between a smirk and a snarl played on the drug dealer's lips.

Francesco's hands clenched into fists. He rose.

The drug dealer turned puce, his belligerence dropping a touch when confronted by Francesco's sheer physical power.

Who makes the rules?

'You are throwing your life away,' he said harshly before turning to Mario. 'Call the police.'

'The police?' squeaked the dealer.

It was obvious that the same question echoed in Mario and his fellow guards' heads.

First the stealing, cheating gambler and now a drug dealer? He could see the consternation on all their faces, could feel them silently wondering if he was going soft.

Naturally, none of his men dared question him verbally, their faces expressionless.

'Yes. The police.' As he walked past the dealer, Francesco added, 'But know that when you're released from your long prison sentence, if I ever find you dealing in drugs again, I will personally break your legs. Take my advice—get yourself an education and go straight.'

With that, he strode out of his office, out of his nightclub, and into the dark Palermo night, oblivious to the cadre of bodyguards who'd snapped into action to keep up with him.

CHAPTER TEN

HANNAH BROUGHT HER bike to a stop outside her small front gate and smothered a yawn. She felt dead on her feet. The Friday-evening traffic had only compounded what had been a *very* long week.

She dismounted and wheeled her bike up the narrow path to her front door. Just as she placed her key in the lock, a loud beep made her turn.

A huge, gleaming black motorbike with an equally huge rider came to a stop right by her front gate.

No way...

Stunned, she watched as Francesco strode towards her, magnificent in his black leathers, removing his helmet, a thunderous look on his face.

'What are you doing here?' Her heart had flown into her mouth and it took all she had not to stand there gaping like a goldfish.

'Never mind that, what the hell are you doing back on that deathtrap?'

He loomed before her, blocking the late sun, his eyes blazing with fury.

Hannah blinked, totally nonplussed at seeing him again. Only years of practice at remaining calm while under fire from distressed patients and their next of kin alike allowed her to retain any composure. 'I don't drive.'

Breathing heavily through his nose, he snapped, 'There are other ways of getting around. I can't believe you're still using this…thing.'

'I'm not. It's a new one.'

'I gathered that, seeing as your old one crumpled like a biscuit tin,' he said, speaking through gritted teeth. 'I'm just struggling to understand why you would still cycle when you nearly died on a bicycle mere weeks ago.'

'I don't like using public transport. Plus, cycling helps shift some of the weight from my bottom,' she added, trying to inject some humour into her tone, hoping to defuse some of the anger still etched on his face. Her attempt failed miserably.

'There is nothing wrong with your bottom,' he said coldly. 'And even if there were—which there isn't—it's hardly worth risking your life for.'

The situation was so surreal Hannah was tempted to pinch herself.

Was she dreaming? She'd had so little sleep since returning from Sicily five days ago that it was quite possible.

'Like every other human on this planet, I could die at any time by any number of accidents. I'm not going to stay off my bike because of one idiot.' She kept her tone firm, making it clear the situation was no longer open for discussion. She was a grown woman. If she wanted to cycle, then that was her business. 'Anyway, you're hardly in a position to judge—do you have any idea the number of mangled motorcyclists I had to patch back together when I was doing my placement in Accident and Emergency?'

A cold snake crawled up her spine at the thought of Francesco being brought in on a trolley….

She blinked the thought away

'My riding skills are second to none, as you know perfectly well,' he said with all the confidence of a man who knew he was the best at what he did. 'In any case, I do not ride around on a piece of cheap tin.'

'You can be incredibly arrogant, did you know that?'

'I've been called much worse, and if being arrogant is what it takes to keep you safe then I can live with that.'

His chocolate eyes held hers with an intensity so deep it almost burned. Her fingers itched to touch him, to rub her thumb over the angry set of his lips.

No matter how…shocked she felt at his sudden appearance, there was something incredibly touching about his anger, knowing it was concern for her safety propelling it.

She looked away, scared to look at him any longer. 'I appreciate your concern, but my safety is not your responsibility.'

Suddenly aware her helmet was still attached to her head, she unclipped it and whipped it off, smoothing her hair down as best she could.

God, since when had she suffered from vanity? Last weekend notwithstanding, not in fifteen years.

And why did she feel an incomprehensible urge to burst into tears?

It was a feeling she'd been stifling since she'd walked back into her home on Sunday night.

'What are you doing here?' she asked again, her cheeks burning as she recalled the two phone calls she'd ignored from him.

'That's not a conversation I wish to have on your doorstep.'

When she made no response, he inclined his head at her door. 'This is the point where you invite me into your home.'

Less than a week ago she'd invited him into her house, only to have him rudely decline.

Then, her heart had hammered with excitement for what

the weekend would bring. Now her heart thrummed just to see *him*…

'Look, you can come in for a little while, but I've had a long, difficult week and a *very* long, *very difficult* day, and I want to get to bed early.' Abruptly, she turned away and opened the door, terrified he would read something of her feelings on her face.

The last word she should be mentioning in front of Francesco was *bed*.

She could hardly credit how naive she'd been in sleeping with him. Had she seriously thought she could share a bed with the sexiest man on the planet and walk away feeling nothing more than a little mild contentment that she'd ticked something off her to-do list?

What a silly, naive fool she'd been.

Francesco thought he'd never been in a more depressing house than the place Hannah called home. It wasn't that there was anything intrinsically wrong with it—on the contrary, it was a pretty two-bedroom house with high ceilings and spacious rooms, but…

There was no feeling to it. Her furniture was minimal and bought for function. The walls were bare of any art or anything that would show the owner's tastes. It was a shell.

Hannah shoved her foldaway bike in a virtually empty cupboard under the stairs and faced him, a look of defiance—and was that fear?—on her face. Her hair had reverted back to its usual unkempt state, a sight that pleased him immeasurably.

'I need a shower,' she said.

'Is that an invitation?' he asked, saying it more as a challenge than from any expectation.

She ignored his innuendo. 'I've been puked on twice today.'

He grimaced. 'So not an invitation.'

'Give me five minutes, then you can tell me whatever it is you came all this way to discuss. While I'm gone, you can make yourself useful by making the coffee.' Thus saying, she headed up the wooden stairs without a backward glance, her peachy bottom showing beautifully in the functional black trousers she wore....

Quickly he averted his eyes. Too much looking at those gorgeous buttocks might just make him climb into that shower with her after all.

Besides, a few minutes to sort their respective heads out would probably be a good idea.

Hannah's reception had not been the most welcoming, but what had he expected? That she would take one look at him and throw herself into his arms?

No, he hadn't expected that. Her silence and polite rebuff by text message had made her feelings clear. Well, tough on her. He was here and they would talk whether she wanted to or not.

Yet there had been no faking the light that had shone briefly in her eyes when she'd first spotted him. It had been mingled with shock, but it had been there, that same light that had beamed straight into his heart the first time she'd opened her eyes to him.

Then he'd ruined it by biting her head off over her bike.

He cursed under his breath. If it took the rest of his life, he'd get her off that deathtrap.

He heard a door close and the sound of running water. Was she naked...?

He inhaled deeply, slung his leather jacket over the post of the stairs, and walked into the small square kitchen. He spotted the kettle easily enough and filled it, then set about finding mugs and coffee.

As he rootled through Hannah's cupboards, his chest slowly constricted.

He had never seen such bare cupboards. The only actual food he found was half a loaf of bread, a box of cereal, a large slice of chocolate cake, and some tomato sauce. And that was it. Nothing else, not even a box of eggs. The fridge wasn't much better, containing some margarine, a pint of milk, and an avocado.

What did she eat?

That question was answered when he opened her freezer.

It wasn't just his chest that felt constricted. His heart felt as if it had been placed in a vice.

The freezer was full. Three trays crammed with ready meals for one.

The ceiling above him creaked, jolting him out of the trance he hadn't realised he'd fallen into.

Experiencing a pang of guilt at rifling through her stuff, he shut the freezer door and went back to the jar of instant coffee he'd found and the small bag of sugar.

No wonder she had wanted to experience a little bit of life.

He'd never met anyone who lived such a solitary existence. Not that anyone would guess. Hannah wasn't antisocial. On the contrary, she was good company. Better than good. Warm, witty… Beautiful. Sexy.

Before too long she emerged to join him in the sparse living room, having changed into a pair of faded jeans and a black T-shirt.

'Your coffee's on the table,' he said, rising from the sofa he'd sat on. He would bet the small dining table in the corner was rarely used for eating on, loaded as it was with medical journals and heaps of paper neatly laid in piles.

'Thank you.' She picked it up and walked past him to

the single seat, leaving a waft of light, fruity fragrance in her wake. She curled up on it, cradling her mug.

Now her eyes met his properly, a brightness glistening from them. 'Francesco, what are you doing here?'

'I want to know why you're avoiding me.'

'I'm not.'

'Don't tell me lies.'

'I haven't seen you to avoid you.'

'You said you were busy this weekend, yet here you are, at home.'

Her head rolled back, her chest rising and falling even more sharply. 'I've only just got back from work, as you well know, and I'm on the rota for tomorrow's night shift. So yes, I am busy.'

'Look at me,' he commanded. He would keep control of his temper if it killed him.

With obvious reluctance, she met his gaze.

'Last weekend… You do realise what we shared was out of this world?'

Her cheeks pinked. 'It was very nice.'

'There are many words to describe it, but *nice* isn't one of them. You and me…'

'There is no you and me,' she blurted, interrupting him. 'I'm sorry to have to put it so crassly, but I don't want to see you again. Last weekend *was* very nice but there will be no repeat performance.'

'You think not?' he said, trying his hardest to keep his tone soft, but when she dug her hand into her pocket and pulled out her phone, the red mist seemed to descend as if from nowhere. 'Do *not* turn that thing on.'

Her eyes widened as if startled before narrowing. 'Don't tell me what I can and can't do. You're not my father.'

'I'm not trying…'

'You certainly are.'

'Will you stop interrupting me?' He raised his voice for the first time.

Her mouth dropped open.

'It's a bit much feeling as if I'm in competition with a phone,' he carried on, uncaring that she had turned a whiter shade of white. He knew without having to be told that there was no competition, because the phone had won without even trying. Because as far as Dr Hannah Chapman was concerned, her phone was all she needed.

He rose to his feet, his anger swelling like an awoken cobra, his venom primed. 'You hide behind it. I bet you sleep with it on your pillow.'

His comment was so close to the mark that Hannah cringed inwardly *and* outwardly. Dear God, why had he come here? Why hadn't he just taken the hint and kept away?

She hadn't asked for any of this. All she'd wanted was to experience one night as a real woman.

She'd ended up with so much more than she'd bargained for.

'Do you really want to spend the rest of your life with nothing but a phone to keep you warm at night?'

'What I want is none of your business,' she said, her tongue running away as she added, 'but just to clarify what I told you in your nightclub, I do *not* want a relationship— not with you, not with anyone.'

He threw his arms out, a sneer on his face. 'Of course you don't want a relationship. Your life is so fulfilling as it is.'

'It is to me.' How she stopped herself screaming that in his face she would never know.

'Look at you. Look at this place. You're hiding away from life. You're like one of those mussels we ate in the casino—you threw yourself at me to experience some of what you'd been missing out on, got what you wanted, then retreated right back into your shell without any thought to the consequences.'

She didn't have a clue what he was talking about. 'What consequences? We used protection.'

'I'm not talking about babies—I'm talking about what you've done to me!' If he'd been a lion he would have roared those last few words, of that she had no doubt. Francesco's fury was a sight to behold, making him appear taller and broader than ever, filling the living room.

She should be terrified. And there was no denying the panic gnawing furiously at the lining of her stomach, but it wasn't fear of him…

No, it was the fear of something far worse.

And this fear put her even further on the defensive.

Shoving her mug on the floor, she jumped to her feet. The calmness she had been wearing as a facade evaporated, leaving her jumbled, terrified emotions raw and exposed. 'I haven't done *anything* to you!'

'You've changed me. I don't know how the hell you did it—maybe you're some kind of witch—but whatever you did, it's real. I let a drug dealer escape without a beating last night, had my men turn him over to the police.'

'And that's a bad thing?'

'It's not how I work. That's never been how I work. Drugs killed my mother. Drug dealers are the scum of the earth and deserve everything they get.' Abruptly he stopped talking and took a long breath in. 'You gave me the best night of my life and I know as well as you do that you enjoyed every minute of it, too. You can deny it until you're blue in the face but we both know what we shared was special. *You* forced that night on *me*. It was what *you* wanted, and it's me that's paying the price for it.'

'You knew it was only for one night.'

'A one-night stand is never that good. Never. Not even close. But now you're treating me as if I'm a plague carrier, and I want to know why.'

'There's nothing to tell. I just don't want to see you again.'

'Will you stop lying?'

'I can't have sex with you again. I just can't. You've screwed with my brain enough as it is.'

'*I've* screwed with *your* brain?' His tone was incredulous. 'Do you have any idea what you've done to *me*?'

'Oh, yes, let's bring it all back to you,' she spat. 'The poor little gangster struggling to deal with his newly found conscience while I…'

Hannah took a deep breath, trying desperately to rein all her emotions back in and under her control. 'After my accident, you filled my mind. You were all I could think about. When I met you it only got worse. I came to you partly because I thought doing something about it would fix it. I thought we would have sex and that would be it—my life would return to normal, I'd be able to go back to concentrating on my job without any outside influences…'

'Didn't it work out exactly as you envisaged?' he asked, his tone mocking.

'No, it did not! I thought it would. But you're still there, filling my head, and I want you gone. My patients deserve all my focus. Every scrap of it. I want to experience more of life, but not to their detriment. This is all *too much* and I can't handle it.'

'I warned you of the consequences,' he said roughly. 'I told you a one-night stand wasn't for a woman like you.'

Something inside Hannah pinged. Taking three paces towards him, she pushed at his chest. 'You are a hypocrite,' she shouted. 'How many women have you used for sex? Double figures? Treble? How many lives have *you* ruined?'

'None. All the women before you knew it would only ever be sex. It meant nothing.'

'Ha! Exactly.' She shoved him again, hard enough to knock him off balance and onto the sofa. 'The minute the tables are turned, your fragile ego can't deal with it...'

She never got to finish her sentence for Francesco grabbed hold of her waist and yanked her onto the sofa with him, pinning her down before she could get a coherent thought in her head.

'You know as well as I do that what we shared meant something,' he said harshly, his hot breath tickling her skin. 'And contrary to your low opinion of my sex life, I am not some kind of male tart. Until last weekend I'd been celibate for ten months.'

She wanted to kick out, scream at him to get off her, but all the words died on her tongue when his mouth came crashing down on hers, a hard, furious kiss that her aching heart and body responded to like a moth to a flame.

That deep masculine taste and scent filled her senses, blocking out all her fears, blocking out everything but him. Francesco.

Just five days away from him, and she had pined. Pined for him. Pined for this.

She practically melted into him, winding her arms around his hard body, clinging to him, pressing every part of her into him.

And he clung to her, too, his hands roaming over her body, bunching her hair, his hot lips grazing her face, her neck, every available bit of flesh.

Being in his arms felt so *right*. Francesco made the coldness that had settled in her bones since she'd returned from Sicily disappear, replacing it with a warmth that seeped through to every part of her.

In a melee of limbs her T-shirt was pulled over her head

and thrown to the floor, quickly followed by Francesco's. Braless, her naked breasts crushed against his chest, the last remaining alarms ringing in her brain vanished and all she could do was savour the feel of his hard strength flush against her.

His strong capable hands playing with the buttons on her jeans, her smaller hands working on the zip of his leathers, somehow they managed to tug both down, using their feet to work them off to join the rest of their strewn clothing, in the process tumbling off the sofa and onto the soft carpet.

Only when they were both naked did Francesco reach for his leathers, pull out his wallet and produce a now familiar square foil.

In a matter of seconds he'd rolled it on and plunged inside her.

This time her body knew exactly what to do. *She* knew exactly what to do. No fears, no insecurities, just pure unadulterated pleasure.

The feel of him, huge inside her, his strength on the verge of crushing her, Hannah let all thoughts fly out of the window, giving in to this most wonderful of all sensations.

Later, lying in the puddle of their clothes on the floor, Francesco's face buried in her neck, his breaths hot against her skin, she opened her eyes and gazed at the ceiling. Hot tears burned the back of her retinas.

'Am I squashing you?' he asked, his breathing still ragged.

'No,' she lied, wrapping her arms even tighter around him.

Francesco lifted his head to look at her. There had been a definite hitch in her voice. 'What's the matter?'

'Nothing.'

'Stop lying to me.'

To his distress, two fat tears rolled down her cheeks.

'I'm so confused. *You* confuse me. I'd told myself I would never sleep with you again and look what's happened. You turn up and I might as well have succumbed to you the moment I let you in the door.'

Rolling onto his back, taking her with him so she rested on his chest, he held her tightly to him. 'All it proves is that we're not over. Not yet. Neither of us wants anything heavy,' he continued. 'For a start, neither of us has the *time* for anything heavy. But we enjoy each other's company, so where's the harm in seeing each other? I promise you, your patients will not suffer for you having a life.'

There was no room for Hannah in his life. Not in any meaningful way. The more he got to know her, the more he knew that what they shared could never be anything more than a fling.

Ever since he'd reached adulthood he'd assumed he would never meet a woman to settle down with. Even before he'd discovered his mother's diaries and learned of his father's despicable behaviour towards her, he'd known how badly she struggled to cope with his father's way of life.

His mother had been a good woman. Kind and loving, even when she was doped to her eyeballs on the drugs his father fed her by the trough. Not that he'd known his father fed them to her—back then he'd believed his father to be as despairing and worried about her habit as he was.

Elisabetta Calvetti had no more fitted into his father's world than Hannah fitted in his.

The women who did fit into Francesco's world and thrived were like poison. The rarer women—women like Hannah who did not fit in—he'd always known should never marry into such a dangerous life. To marry into it would destroy them, just as it had destroyed his mother.

Deep down, he knew he should have accepted her rebuffs and left her alone, but the past few days...

How could he concentrate on anything when his mind was full of Hannah?

The wolves, in the form of Luca Mastrangelo, were circling the Mayfair casino and Francesco needed to be on the ball. Otherwise the deal that would symbolise above all others that Salvatore Calvetti's empire was over, his legacy shrivelled to dust, would be lost.

He wasn't ready to let her go. Not yet. Knowing Hannah was in his life meant he could focus his attention entirely on the purchase of the casino and not have his mind filled with her.

'Okay,' she said slowly, pressing a kiss to his chest. 'As long as you promise not to make any demands on my time when I'm working, we can see each other.'

His arms tightened while the constriction in his chest loosened. He ignored the fact that her condition for seeing him—a condition he was used to dictating to his lovers and not the other way round—made his throat fill with bile.

CHAPTER ELEVEN

THE MAYFAIR CASINO was a lot shabbier than the ones Francesco owned, but the decoration was not something that concerned him. That was cosmetic and easily fixed. Even the accounts, usually his first consideration when buying a new business, mattered not at all. All he craved was what the business symbolised.

Tonight, though, symbolism and everything else could take a hike. He'd finally managed to drag Hannah out for the night.

Naturally, she'd been too busy to buy a new dress and had changed into the same dress she'd worn three weeks before in Sicily, confessing with an embarrassed smile that it was the only suitable item in her wardrobe.

He'd bitten back the offer of buying her a whole new wardrobe. He knew without having to ask that she would refuse. He was man enough to admit that it had been a blow to his pride when he'd learned she'd paid for the dress herself in Palermo. And her haircut. It surprised him, though, how much he respected her for it. She'd had free rein in that boutique. She could have easily racked up a bill for tens of thousands of euros, all in his name.

Tonight she looked beautiful. In the ten minutes she'd taken to get changed, she'd brushed her hair, but all this had done was bush it out even more. She'd applied only a little make-up. All she wore on her feet were her black ballet slippers.

In Francesco's eyes she looked far more ravishing than she had three weeks ago when she'd gone the whole nine yards with her appearance. Now she looked real. She looked like Hannah.

An elderly man with salt-and-pepper hair ambled towards them, his hand outstretched. 'Francesco, I didn't know you would be joining us this evening.' There was a definite tremor in both his hand and voice.

'I wanted to show my guest around the place,' he replied, shaking the wizened hand before introducing him to Hannah. 'This is Dr Hannah Chapman. Hannah, this is Sir Godfrey Renfrew, the current owner of this establishment.'

'Doctor?' Godfrey's eyes swept her up and down, a hint of confusion in them.

'Lovely to meet you,' Hannah said, smiling. Did Francesco *have* to keep referring to her by her title?

'The pleasure is mine,' he said quickly, before fixing his attention back on Francesco. 'I have some of your compatriots visiting me this evening.'

So that was the reason for Godfrey's discomfort.

Francesco glanced around the room, homing in on two tall men leaning against a far wall drinking beer.

So his spies had been onto something when they'd reported that Luca Mastrangelo was trying to usurp the deal. And it seemed as if Pepe was in on it, too.

If Francesco was in Sicily, all he would have to do was whisper a few well-chosen words into Godfrey's ear and the casino would be his.

But he wasn't in Sicily. And Godfrey had already proved himself immune to Sicilian threats, and much worse.

'I see them,' Francesco confirmed, keeping his tone steady, bored, even. 'They're old acquaintances of mine.'

'Yes...they said you had...history.'

That was one way of describing it. Smiling tightly, he bowed his head. 'I should go and say hello.'

Now wishing he hadn't brought Hannah out with him, Francesco bore her off towards the Mastrangelo brothers.

'Who are we going to say hello to?' she asked, surprising him by slipping her fingers through his.

Apart from when they were lying in bed together, she never held his hand. Not that they'd ever actually been out anywhere to hold hands, all their time together over the past fortnight having been spent eating takeaway food and making love.

'Old acquaintances of mine,' he said tightly, although the feel of her gentle fingers laced through his had a strangely calming reaction.

By the time they stood before the Mastrangelo brothers, his stomach felt a fraction more settled.

'Luca. Pepe.' He extended his hand. 'So the rumours are true,' he said, switching to Sicilian.

'What rumours would they be?' asked Luca, shaking his hand with a too-firm grip. Francesco squeezed a little tighter in turn before dropping the hold.

'I'd heard you were interested in this place.'

Luca shrugged.

'I thought you'd got out of the casino game.'

'Times change.'

'Clearly.' Francesco forced a smile. 'Does your little wife know you're going back into forbidden territory?'

Luca bared his teeth. 'You leave Grace out of this.'

'I wouldn't dream of bringing her into it, knowing how much she hates me.' Here, he looked at Pepe. 'I do believe your sister-in-law hates me more than you do.' Not giving either of them the chance to respond, he flashed his own teeth. 'I suggest the pair of you rethink your decision to try to buy this place. The documents for my ownership are on the verge of completion.'

Pepe finally spoke. 'But they're not completed yet, are they?'

'They will be soon. And if either of you try anything to stop the sale going through, you will live to regret it.'

'Are you threatening us?'

'You sound surprised, Luca,' he said, deliberately keeping his tone amicable. 'You should know I am not a man to deal with threats. Only promises.'

Luca pulled himself to his full height. 'I will not be threatened, Calvetti. Remember that.'

Only the gentle squeeze of Hannah's fingers lacing back through his stopped Francesco squaring up to his old friend.

He shook himself. He didn't want to be having this conversation in front of her, regardless of the fact that they were speaking in their native tongue and not in English.

'Don't start a war you'll never win, Mastrangelo.'

'I remember your father saying exactly the same thing to me when my father died. Your father thought he could take control of the Mastrangelo estate.' Luca smiled. 'He didn't succeed in getting his way. And nor will you.'

Baring his teeth one last time, Francesco said, 'But I am not my father. I have infinitely more patience.'

'Are you okay?' Hannah asked as soon as they were out of earshot.

'I'm fine. Let's get out of here.'

'But we've only just arrived.'

Expelling air slowly through his nose, he stopped himself from insisting they leave right now. He could insist and she would have no choice but to follow, but to do so would upset her, and that was the last thing he wanted to do.

Strangely enough, Hannah's presence tempered the

angry adrenaline flowing through him—not by much, but enough to take the edge off it.

Having promised to teach her how to play Blackjack, he found seats at a table for them to join in. Unlike at the tournament in Sicily, where her remarkable poker face was her biggest asset, there was no bluffing needed when playing against the dealer. She still picked it up like a pro. At one point he thought she would finish with more chips than him.

Watching her have fun eased a little more of his rage, enough so that there were moments he forgot the Mastrangelos were there, trying to muscle in on his territory. It pleased him enormously to watch her drink a full glass of champagne. She really was learning to switch off.

His driver was ready for them when they left. As soon as they were seated in the back, the partition separating them from the driver, Hannah squished right next to him and reached for his hand. Pulling it onto her lap, she rubbed her thumb in light circular motions over his inner wrist.

The breath of air he inhaled went into his lungs that bit easier.

'How do you know those two men?' she asked after a few moments of silence.

He could only respect her reticence in waiting until they were alone before starting her cross-examination. 'Luca and Pepe?'

'Is that their names?' she said drily. 'You forgot to introduce us.'

He sighed. 'I apologise. They're old friends. Were old friends. At least, Luca was.'

'Was?'

'Their father used to work for my father. And then he quit.'

He felt her blanch.

'Don't worry. My father didn't touch him—they'd been

childhood friends themselves, which saved Pietro from my father's vengeance. But the fact my father didn't put a bullet through him didn't mean the perceived slur could be forgotten. Once their professional relationship finished, family loyalty meant any friendship between Luca and I was finished, too. It's all about respect.' In his father's eyes, everything had been about respect. Everything.

How he'd envied the easy affection the two Mastrangelo boys shared with their father. It was the kind of relationship he'd longed for, but for Salvatore Calvetti a sign of affection for his only child consisted of a slap on the back if he pleased him.

'Have you not seen Luca since then?'

'He came to my father's funeral.' He looked away, not wanting her to see the expression on his face reflecting what he felt beneath his skin whenever he thought of his father's funeral. While a tiny part of him had felt relief that he could break free from Salvatore's shadow, he'd mourned the man. Truly mourned him.

If he'd known then what he knew now, he would have lit fireworks by his open graveside in celebration.

'My father's death freed me. It freed Luca and me to resume our old friendship. When we were kids we often used to play cards together, and always said that when we grew up we would open a casino together. We opened our first one three years ago, but then last year he decided he wanted out.'

'Why was that?'

He met her eyes. 'His wife thought I was bad for him.'

Her forehead furrowed. 'He said that?'

'Not in so many words. But it was obvious. She hates my guts.'

Still her forehead furrowed. 'But why?'

'Because I'm a big bad gangster.'

'No, your father was a big bad gangster,' she corrected.

'Even after everything you've witnessed, you still refuse to see it.' He planted a kiss on the end of her nose.

'No, I *do* see it. You are who you are, but you're nowhere near as bad as you like people to think.'

She wouldn't say that if she could read the thoughts going through his mind. Thoughts of revenge, not just against his father but against Luca Mastrangelo. And Pepe.

He would not allow the Mayfair casino to fall into Mastrangelo hands. It was *his* and he would do whatever was needed to ensure it.

'Do I take it that those men are also interested in buying the casino?' Hannah asked, swinging her legs onto his lap.

'I'd heard rumours they were after it. Being there tonight confirmed it.'

'And do I take it you threatened them?' At his surprised glance, she grinned ruefully. 'I might not speak Sicilian, but I can read body language.'

'And you think I have *good* in me?' Rubbing his hand absently over her calf, he couldn't help but notice the little bags that had formed under her eyes. Those little bags made his heart constrict.

This was a woman who worked so hard for such a good purpose she hardly slept. And *she* saw good in *him*?

'You won't hurt them,' she said with simple confidence.

He didn't answer. The one thing he would never do was lie to her. He'd lived a lifetime of lies.

Before she could question his silence, her phone vibrated. Dropping his hand, she reached into her bag.

'Is it work?' he asked, trying hard to keep the edge from his voice. The only time Hannah lost her sweet humour was when he mentioned her excessive use of her phone. On those occasions her claws came out.

She shook her head absently. 'Melanie.'

'She's back from her work trip?'

'Yep. She wants to know if I'm free tomorrow for the last fitting. For my bridesmaid dress,' she added heavily.

'Are you not going to answer?' When it came to work she would fire off a reply the second she read them.

'I suppose I should.'

Before he could question her reluctance, they pulled up outside his hotel.

'Shall we have a bath together?' he asked once they were safely ensconced in his suite.

Hannah's nose wrinkled. She felt all…out of sorts. Right then she needed something sweet to counteract the acidity that had formed in her throat. 'Can we have chocolate-fudge cake first?'

'Hot?'

She smiled. Already he knew her so well. Especially with regard to her hot chocolate-fudge cake addiction, which was fast becoming usurped by her Francesco addiction.

Was this how drug addicts started out? she wondered. A little fix here, a little fix there, then swearing never to do it again? But then temptation was placed right under their nose and they were too weak to resist? Because that was how she felt with him. Unable to resist.

Why did she even need to keep resisting? Addictions were bad things. How could Francesco possibly be classed as bad for her? Her work hadn't suffered for being with him.

The only reason to resist now was for the sake of her heart, and she'd already lost that battle. In reality, she hadn't stood a chance.

She looked at him, her big bear of a man.

What would he say if he knew that, despite all her protestations over not wanting a relationship, she'd fallen for him?

She'd watched him square up to those two men in the

casino and she'd wanted to dive between them and kung fu them into keeping away from him.

The strength of her protectiveness towards him had shocked her.

It was how she used to be with Beth. If you messed with one twin you messed with the other.

And like it had been with Beth, when she was with Francesco she felt safe. She felt complete. It was a different completeness but every bit as powerful.

'Will you come to Melanie's wedding with me?' She blurted out the words before she'd even properly thought of them.

Her heart lurched to see the palpable shock on his face.

'Sorry. Forget I said anything,' she said quickly. 'It's a silly…'

'You took me by surprise, that's all,' he cut in with a shake of his head. 'You want me to come to your sister's wedding?'

'Only if you're not too busy. I just…' She bit her lip. 'I just could do with…'

Francesco didn't know what she was trying to tell him, but the darting of her eyes and the way she wrung her hands together pierced something in him.

'Will there be room for me?' he asked, stalling for time while he tried to think.

A sound like a laugh spluttered from her lips. 'If I tell them I'm bringing a date they'll make room, even if it means sitting one of the grandparents on someone else's lap.'

'Okay,' he agreed, injecting more positivity than he felt inside. 'I'll come with you.'

The gratitude in her eyes pierced him even deeper.

It wasn't until midmorning they got into the enormous bath together. After a night of making love and snatches of tortured sleep, Hannah was happy to simply lie between Francesco's legs, her head resting against his chest, and enjoy the bubbly water.

Her phone, which she'd placed on the shelf above the sink, vibrated.

'Leave it,' he commanded, tightening his hold around her waist.

'It might be important.'

'It will still be there in ten minutes.'

'But…'

'Hannah, this can't continue. You're using your phone as an emotional crutch and it's not good for you.' There was a definite sharpness to his tone.

Since they'd started seeing each other properly, she'd been acutely aware of his loathing for her phone. Not her work, or the research papers or her studying; just her phone.

'I think it's a bit much you calling it an emotional crutch,' she said tightly. 'If one of my patients dies when I'm not on shift, then I want to know—I don't want to get to work and come face-to-face with bereaved parents in the car park or atrium or café or wherever and not know that they've just lost the most precious thing in their lives.'

The edge to his voice vanished. 'Is that what happened to you when Beth died?'

She jerked a nod. 'When Beth was first admitted, the doctor was very clinical in his approach, almost cold.' She fixed her gaze on Francesco's beautiful arms, adoring the way the water darkened the hair and flattened it over the olive skin. 'Beth died in the early hours of the morning, long after that first doctor had finished his shift. Luckily, she was in the care of some of the loveliest, most compassionate doctors and nurses you could wish for. They let us stay with her body for hours, right until the sun came up. I remember we had to go back to the children's ward as we'd left Beth's possessions there when she'd been taken off to Intensive Care. We got into the lift and that first doctor got in with us.'

She paused, swallowing away the acrid bile that formed in her throat.

'He looked right through us. Either he didn't recognise us as the family of the young girl he'd been treating twenty-four hours before, or he did recognise us and just didn't want to acknowledge us. Either way, I hated him for it. My sister was dead and that man didn't even care enough to remember our faces.'

'Do you still hate him?'

She shook her head. 'I understand it now. There are only so many times you can watch a child die before you grow a hard shell. We all do it. The difference is, he let his shell consume him at the expense of the patient. I will *never* allow myself to become like that. I never want any of my patients or their loved ones to think I don't care.'

'That must take its toll on you, though,' he observed. Francesco had only watched one person die: his mother. He'd made it to the hospital in time to say goodbye, but by that point the essence of *her* had already gone, her body kept alive by machines.

It had been the single most distressing event of his life.

To choose a profession where you were surrounded by illness and death... He could hardly begin to comprehend the dedication and selflessness needed to do such a job.

She shrugged, but her grip on his arms tightened. 'We send hundreds more children home healed than we lose. That more than makes up for it.'

He found himself at a loss for what to say.

Hannah had suffered the loss of the most precious person in her life—her twin—and she'd turned her grief into a force for good.

Hadn't he known from the start that she was too good for him? He still knew it, more than ever.

'Beth's death broke something inside me,' she said quietly. 'My parents tried very hard to comfort me, but they were grieving, too, and in any case I pushed them away. Melanie was desperate to comfort me, but I pushed her away, too. Since my accident I can see how badly I've treated my family. I've kept myself apart from them. I've kept myself apart from everyone...until you.'

His chest tightened. 'Your family was happy for you to isolate yourself?'

'No.' Her damp hair tickled his nose. 'They weren't happy. But what could they do about it? They couldn't *make* me.' Her voice became wistful. 'I think I wanted them to force the issue. I was so lost but I couldn't find the way out....'

There was so much Francesco wanted to say as her words trailed away. None of it would help.

'You're probably right about my phone,' she muttered. 'I guess I have been using it as a crutch. It's easier for me to interact with an object than a human. At least that was the case until I met you.'

She turned her head, resting her cheek on his shoulder as she stared at him. 'I'm so glad you're coming to the wedding with me.'

The very mention of the *W* word was enough to make his stomach roil.

'I've been dreading it for so long now,' she confessed.

'Is Beth the reason you're so anxious about it?' He dragged his question out. 'Because she can't be there?'

Her nails dug into his arms. 'This is the first real family event we've had since she died.' She placed a kiss to his neck and inhaled. 'With you by my side, I think I can endure it without ruining Melanie's day. The last thing I want is to spoil things for her, but I don't think even my poker face will be able to hide my feelings.' She swallowed. 'It's all feeling so raw again.'

Francesco cleared the sourness forming in his throat.

He hadn't bargained on this. None of it was part of his plan, whereby he would see her whilst spending lots of time in London finalising the Mayfair deal, after which they would head their separate ways.

None of this was in the script.

He hadn't for a minute imagined she would start needing him, not his self-sufficient doctor who didn't rely on anyone but herself.

Something gripped at his chest, a kind of panic.

If it wasn't for the tears spilling down her cheeks and the confidences she'd just entrusted him with, he would have dreamed up a good excuse not to go there and then.

But Hannah crying? In his mind there was no worse sight or sound. He would promise her anything to stop it.

Francesco slammed his phone down in fury.

The purchase agreement he'd spent months working on had been blown out of the water, with Godfrey Renfrew admitting he wanted time to 'consider an alternative offer'.

The Mastrangelos were standing in his way.

He picked the receiver up and dialled his lawyer's number. 'I want you to arrange a meeting between me and Luca Mastrangelo,' he said, his words delivered like ice picks. 'Tell him that unless he agrees to meet tomorrow, he will only have himself to blame for the consequences.'

The second he put the phone down, his mobile rang. It was Hannah. *'Ciao,'* he said, breathing heavily through his teeth.

'What's the matter?' she asked, picking up on his tone even though she was in London and he in Palermo.

'Nothing. I'm just busy. What can I do for you?' Looking at the clock on his wall, he could see it was lunchtime. She must be calling him on her break.

'I haven't heard from you in a couple of days. I just wanted to make sure you're okay.' There wasn't any accusation in her voice. All he heard was concern.

'I'm busy, that's all.'

Silence, then, 'Any idea what time you'll be over tomorrow?'

He rubbed his eyes. He'd promised he'd be back in London early Friday evening so they could head straight down to Devon. She'd even booked him a hotel room.

'I'll confirm tomorrow morning,' he said, wishing he could relieve the sharp pain digging in the back of his eyes. He would ensure his meeting with Luca and Pepe took place in the morning. That would give him plenty of time to get to her.

More silence. 'Are you sure you're okay?'

'Go back to your patients, Dr Chapman. I'll see you tomorrow.'

Hannah checked her watch for the umpteenth time. Her bags were all packed, butterflies playing merry havoc in her belly.

She felt sick with nerves and dread. Knowing Francesco would be by her side throughout it all dulled it a little but not as much as it should.

He'd sounded so distant on the phone. The plentiful text messages from him had whittled away to nothing.

Something niggled in her stomach, a foreboding she was too scared to analyse.

Twitching her curtain, relief poured through her to see the large black car pull up outside.

Her relief was short-lived when she opened the door

and saw the serious look on his face. 'You're not coming with me, are you?'

He stepped over the threshold and pushed the door shut behind him. 'I apologise for the short notice, but I have to meet with Luca and Pepe Mastrangelo tomorrow lunchtime. The sale of the Mayfair casino is under threat.'

For long moments she did nothing but stare at him. 'You bastard.'

He flinched, but a cold hostility set over his features. 'I do not have the power to be in two places at once. If I could then I would.'

'Liar,' she stated flatly, although her chest had tightened so much she struggled to find breath.

This could not be happening.

'You could have arranged the meeting for any time you like. Your life doesn't revolve around a set schedule.' Francesco's time was his to do as he pleased. One of the very things she'd been so attracted to had turned around and bitten her hard.

Francesco could do as he liked, and what he liked was to avoid her sister's wedding.

He was asking her to face it alone.

After everything she had confided and all the trust she'd placed in him, he was leaving her to face the wedding on her own.

'It has to be tomorrow.' He raked his hands through his hair. 'I wanted to organise it for today but tomorrow is the only day the three of us can be in the same country at the same time. Time is of the essence. I won't allow the Mastrangelos to steal the casino away from me. I've worked too long on the deal to let it slip through my fingers—it's far too important for me to lose. I've arranged for Mario to drive you to Devon.'

'Don't bother. I'll make my own way there.' She'd

rather cycle on her pushbike. She'd rather walk. 'You can leave now.'

'Hannah, I know you're disappointed. I've gone out of my way to tell you personally—'

'Well, that makes everything all right, then,' she snapped. 'You're blowing me out of the water so you can kneecap some old friends but, hey, no worries, *you told me to my face.*'

'I have spent the best part of a year demolishing my father's empire, eradicating the streets from the evils he peddled,' Francesco said, his voice rising, his cool facade disappearing before her eyes. 'The only business he wanted that he couldn't have was this casino. He did everything in his power to get it, including abducting Godfrey's son, and still he didn't win. But *I will*. It's taken me *months* to gain Godfrey's trust and I will not allow the Mastrangelos to snatch it away from me.'

His father? Hannah had known his relationship with his dead father had been difficult, had seen the way he tensed whenever Salvatore was mentioned, but she'd never suspected the depths of Francesco's animosity towards him.

He paused, his eyes a dark pit of loathing, his malevolence a living, breathing thing. 'You live your life imagining Beth watching over you. Well, I imagine mine with my father watching over me. I like the thought of him staring down watching me destroy everything he built, but more than anything I want him to see me succeed where he failed. I want him turning in his hellish coffin.'

Hannah didn't think she had ever witnessed such hatred before, a loathing that crawled under her skin and settled in the nauseous pit of her belly.

This was the Francesco he had warned her about right at the start. The Francesco she had refused to see.

And now she did see, all she felt was a burning anger that made her want to throw up.

'Go and take your vengeance. Go ruin your old friends. Go and show your dead father how much *better* you are than him by purchasing the very casino he could never have. Let it symbolise how *different* you are to him.'

Shoving him out of the way, she opened the front door. 'Now leave, and don't you *ever* contact me again.'

His chest heaving, he stared at her before his nostrils flared and he strode past her.

'Enjoy your vengeance, Francesco,' she spat. 'Try not to let it choke you.'

He didn't look back.

CHAPTER TWELVE

HANNAH FIXED THE back of her pearl earrings into place, trying desperately hard to contain her shaking hands. Since that awful confrontation with Francesco the night before, it had been a constant battle to stop the tremors racking through her. The long last-minute train journey to Devon had been a constant battle, too—a battle to stop any tears forming for the bastard who'd abandoned her when she needed him most.

She didn't want to think about him. Not now. Not when she was minutes away from leaving for the church to watch her little sister get married.

There was a tap on the door, and Melanie walked into the room carrying a small box.

'How do I look?' she asked, putting the box on the floor, extending her arms and giving a slow twirl.

'Oh, Mel, you look beautiful.' And she did, an angel in white.

'You look beautiful, too.' Careful not to crease each other's dresses—Hannah wore a baby-pink bridesmaid dress—they embraced, then stepped back from each other.

'The cars are here and our bouquets are ready,' Melanie said. Her eyes fixed on Hannah's bedside table, on which rested a photo of Hannah and Beth, aged eight. 'I've got a bouquet for her, too.'

'What do you mean?'

'Beth. I've got her a bouquet, too.'

Hannah had to strain to hear her sister's voice.

'If she was still here she'd be a bridesmaid with you.' A look of mischief suddenly crossed Melanie's face. 'The pair of you would probably follow me down the aisle trying to trip me up.'

A burst of mirth spluttered from Hannah's mouth. She and Beth together had been irrepressible. 'We were really mean to you.'

'No, you weren't.'

'Yes, we were. We hardly ever let you play with us and when we did it was to torment you. I remember we convinced you to let us make you into a princess.'

'Oh, yes! You coloured my hair pink with your felt tip pens and used red crayon as blusher. You treated me like a doll.'

'I'm sorry.'

'Don't be. I was just happy you wanted to play with me.'

'It must have been hard for you, though,' Hannah said, thinking of all the times Melanie had been desperate to join in with their games, how their mum would force them to let her tag along and they would spend the whole time ignoring her. Unless they found a good use for her.

Melanie didn't even pretend not to understand. 'It was hard. I was very jealous. You had each other. You didn't need me.'

Silence rent the room as they both stared at the photo. Despite all her vows, hot tears stung the back of Hannah's eyes. How desperately she wished Beth was there. And how desperately the pathetic side of her wished Francesco was there, too....

Thank God Melanie hadn't grilled her about the latest sudden change to the seating plan, simply giving her a quick hug and a 'No problem.'

Melanie cleared her throat. 'We should get going before we ruin our make-up.'

Looking at her, Hannah could see Melanie's eyes had filled, too, a solitary tear trickling down her cheek.

She reached over to wipe it away with her thumb, then pressed a kiss to her sister's cheek. 'You do look beautiful, Mel. Beth would be insanely jealous.'

Melanie laughed and snatched a tissue from the box on Hannah's bedside table. She blew her nose noisily, then crouched down to the box she'd brought in and removed the lid. 'Here's your bouquet, and here's the one for Beth. I thought you might like to give it to her.'

Hannah sniffed the delicate fragrance.

She looked at her sister. Melanie had been nine when Beth died. A little girl. Now she was a woman less than an hour away from marriage.

How had she missed her own sister growing up? It had happened right before her eyes and she'd been oblivious to it. Melanie had followed Hannah to London. She had been the one to keep the sisterly relationship going—she'd been the one who'd kept the whole family going. Unlike their parents, who still took Hannah's reclusiveness at face value, Melanie at least tried. It was always at her suggestion that they would go out for lunch. It was always Melanie who organised their monthly visits back to Devon, carefully selecting the weekends Hannah wasn't on shift. Melanie, who had never wanted anything more than the company of her big sister.

Her sister. The same flesh and blood as herself and Beth.

Hannah took another sniff of the flowers. 'Do you want to come with me and give them to her?'

'Really?' Melanie was too sweet to even pretend to fake nonchalance.

When it came to visiting Beth, Hannah preferred solitude. Alone, she could chat to her and fill her in on all the family and work gossip.

Since the funeral she had never visited with anyone else. She had done far too many things alone.

All those wasted years hiding herself away, too numb from the pain of her broken heart to even consider letting anyone in—not her parents, not her sister. No one. And she hadn't even realised she was doing it, pretending to be content in her little cocoon.

She hadn't meant to let Francesco in. If she'd known the risk to her heart, she would have taken his advice at the first turn and found a safer method to start living her life.

But she had let him in. In return he'd dumped her in the cruellest of fashions.

She didn't care about his reasons. He'd left her to face this day alone and she would never forgive him.

Except she wasn't alone....

Her heart had opened for him, but it had also opened for her poor neglected family, who wanted nothing more than to love her. All those years spent hiding her heart from them had been wasted years, she could see that now.

She didn't want to hide any more. She couldn't. She needed them. She *loved* them.

Ironically, Francesco's rejection had helped in an unexpected fashion. She would *not* allow Melanie's big day to be ruined by *him*.

Fixing her old practised smile to her face, she took Melanie's hand in her own and gave it a squeeze. 'Why don't we leave now? We can do it before the ceremony starts.'

Melanie's eyes shone. 'I would really like that.'

'Beth would, too. And so would I.'

* * *

Francesco checked his watch. It was bang on half past one.

In thirty minutes Melanie Chapman would walk down the aisle, followed by her doctor sister.

He swatted the thought away.

Now was not the time to be wondering how Hannah was holding up.

Now was the time for action.

With Mario and Roberto by his side, he strolled through the lobby of the neutral hotel both parties had agreed upon and headed up in the lift to the private suite hired for the occasion.

Two men, equally as large as his own minders, guarded the door.

'Wait here,' he said to his men.

This conversation was private.

Sweeping past them, he stepped into the room and shut the door.

He could taste the malice in the air in his first inhalation.

Luca sat at the long dining table, his black eyes fixing on him.

Pepe leant against a wall, his arms folded.

Hannah would be on her way to the church...

Where had that thought come from?

He'd successfully pushed Hannah out of his mind since he'd left her home. He'd cut her out. He would *not* allow himself to think of her. Or the pain on her face. Or the words she'd said, her implication that he was exactly like his father.

He was not like his father.

If he was anything like his father, Luca and Pepe would both be long dead by now—Pepe when he'd tried to fight him all those years ago, Luca when he'd broken their partnership. He hadn't just broken their partnership, he'd severed their friendship, too.

'Well?' said Luca, breaking the silence. 'You're the one who wanted this meeting. What do you want, Calvetti?'

He'd thought he'd known. The casino. The final piece in the obliteration of Salvatore Calvetti's legacy.

His revenge against the man Francesco had learned too late had used his mother as a punchbag.

As hard as he tried to push her out, the only image in his head was Hannah, lying on the cold concrete and opening her eyes, that serene smile that had stolen his breath.

Stolen his heart.

'Well?' Luca's voice rose. 'What do you want?'

Francesco looked at the two brothers. His old friends. He looked at Pepe, the man whose girlfriend he'd stolen all those years ago. He hadn't known she was still seeing him, but he'd known damn well Pepe had been serious about her.

No wonder Pepe hated him.

He looked back at Luca. His oldest friend. A man who'd found that rare kind of love he would do anything to keep.

The rare kind of love he could have with Hannah.

Could have had if he hadn't abandoned her on the one day she needed him.

He'd known the second she'd asked him to go to the wedding with her that she'd fallen for him.

And he, stupid fool that he was, had thrown it back in her face so cruelly, and for what?

Vengeance against a man who was already rotting in hell.

His heart beat so loudly a drum could have been in his ear.

Hannah wasn't his mother. She wasn't a young, suggestible girl. She was a professional woman with more backbone than anyone he knew.

More important, he wasn't his father, something she'd known from the off.

Only two people in his entire life had looked at him and seen *him*, Francesco, and not just Salvatore's son. One of those had given birth to him. The other was at that very moment bleeding with pain for her dead twin who couldn't be there to celebrate their sister's marriage.

What had he done?

He took a step back and raised his hands. 'It's yours.' At their identical furrowed brows, he allowed the tiniest of smiles to form on his lips. 'The casino. If you want it so badly, you can have it.'

They exchanged glances, their bodies straightening.

'I'm serious. It's all yours. I'll call Godfrey and withdraw my offer.' When he reached the door he looked straight at Pepe. 'I was very sorry to hear about the loss of your baby.'

Pepe's eyes flickered.

Turning back to Luca, Francesco continued, 'Send my regards to Grace. She's far too good for you, but I think you already know that.'

He turned the handle of the door.

'Calvetti.' It was Luca's voice.

Francesco turned one last time.

'The casino's yours. Not ours.'

'Sorry?'

A rueful grin spread over Luca's face. 'Grace and Cara were already furious at us for looking at buying a casino, and they're just about ready to kill us for instigating a war with you. We've already told Godfrey to accept your offer.'

In spite of the agonies going on within him, Francesco managed a grin. 'See? I said Grace was too good for you.'

Just as Hannah was too good for him.

He looked at his watch again. At any moment the bridal party would start their slow walk down the aisle.

'I need to be somewhere.'

Hannah followed Melanie up the aisle, trying very hard to keep a straight face, a hard job considering the train of Melanie's dress was streaked with grass and mud.

Beth was buried in the cemetery attached to this very church, and the pair had left the rest of the bridal party to say a few words to her and leave the bouquet by her headstone.

All those years when she'd refused to visit Beth's grave with anyone... How selfish she'd been.

How glad she was that Melanie had found a man who put her first, who loved her enough to compensate for all the neglect she had suffered at the hands of her big sister. Not that Melanie saw it as neglect. Bless her heart, Melanie understood. It hadn't been said, not in so many words, but it didn't need to be.

In all the years Hannah had been grieving the loss of her twin, she had neglected to recognise there was another person in her life grieving, too—a young woman who was a part of her, just as Beth was. Sure, it wasn't exactly the same—how could it be? But then, what two relationships were ever the same? Their parents loved them equally but the relationships between them all were different. Hannah's relationship with them couldn't be any more different.

She looked at her father, walking with Melanie's arm tucked inside his. She might not be able to see his face but she could perfectly imagine the radiant smile on his face. And there was her mother, on her feet in a front pew, still a beautiful woman, looking from her beloved husband to her two surviving daughters, tears already leaking down her cheeks.

And there was the groom, his legs bouncing, his nerves

and excitement palpable. When he knelt before the priest by the side of his fiancée, titters echoed throughout the church at the *HE* written in white on the sole of his left shoe, and the *LP* on the right.

So much love. So much excitement for a new life being forged together.

As they exchanged their vows, the tears she'd successfully kept at bay since that terrible argument with Francesco broke free.

According to Francesco's satnav, the route from London to Devon should take three hours and forty-five minutes by car. By motorbike, he estimated he could make it in two hours.

What he hadn't accounted for was stationary traffic as hordes of holidaymakers took advantage of the late English summer to head to the coast.

This was a country of imbeciles, he thought scathingly as he snaked his way around motionless cars. Why couldn't they all be sensible like Hannah and travel down on the Friday night when the roads were empty?

The ceremony would be over by now, the wedding breakfast in full swing.

Hannah needed air. Her lungs felt too tight.

She'd tried. She really had. She'd smiled throughout the ceremony and wedding breakfast, held pleasant conversations with countless family members and old friends she hadn't seen in years. The number-one question she'd received was a variant of 'Have you met a nice man yet?' While she'd answered gracefully, 'Not yet, but I'm sure I will one day,' each time she was asked it felt as if a thorn were being pressed deep into her heart.

Now all the guests had congregated at the bar while the

function room was transformed for the evening bash, she saw her opportunity for escape.

She stepped out into the early-evening dusk and sat on a bench in the hotel garden. She closed her eyes, welcoming the slight breeze on her face.

Five minutes. That was all she needed. Five minutes of solitude to clamp back down on her emotions.

'Can I join you?'

Opening her eyes, she found her mother standing before her.

Unable to speak, she nodded.

'It's been a beautiful day,' her mum commented.

Hannah nodded again, scared to open her mouth lest she would no longer be able to hold on.

How could Francesco have left her alone like this?

How could she have got him so wrong?

She'd been so convinced he would never hurt her.

She'd been right about the physical aspect. In that respect he'd given her nothing but pleasure. Emotionally, though… he'd ripped her apart.

For the first time in fifteen years she'd reached out to someone for help. He'd known what a massive thing that was for her and still he'd abandoned her, and for what? For revenge on someone who wasn't even alive to see it.

Had she been too needy? Was that it? How could she know? She had nothing to compare it to. Until she'd barged her way into his life, she'd had no form of a relationship with anyone. Not even her family. Not since Beth…

'Why did you let me hide away after Beth died?' she asked suddenly. Francesco's probing questions about her relationship with her parents had been playing on her mind, making her question so many things she'd never considered before.

She felt her mother start beside her.

A long silence formed until her mum took Hannah's hand into her own tentatively, as if waiting for Hannah to snatch it away. 'That's a question your father and I often ask. When Beth died, we knew, no matter the pain we were going through and Mel was going through, that it was nothing compared to what you were living with. You and Beth… you were two peas in a pod. She was you and you were her.'

Hannah's chin wobbled.

'When you said you wanted to be a doctor, we were happy you had something to focus on. When you first hid yourself away, saying you were studying, we thought it was a good thing.' She rummaged in her handbag for a tissue and dabbed her eyes. 'We should have handled it better. We were all grieving, but we should never have allowed you to cut yourself off. At the time, though, we couldn't see it. It was so gradual that by the time we realised how isolated you'd become, we didn't know how to reach out to you anymore. To be honest, I still don't. I wish I could turn the clock back to your teenage years and insist you be a part of the family and not some lodger who shared the occasional meal with us.'

'I wish I could, too,' Hannah whispered. She gazed up at the emerging stars, then turned to look at her mother. 'Mum, can I have a hug?'

Her mum closed her eyes as if in prayer before pulling Hannah into her embrace, enveloping her tightly in that remembered mummy smell that comforted her more than any word could.

Hannah swallowed the last of her champagne. The bubbles playing on her tongue reminded her of Francesco. The optics behind the bar reminded her of Francesco. The man who'd just stepped into the function room, where the dancing was now in full swing, also reminded her of Francesco.

Unable to bear the reminder, she turned her attention back to the party surrounding her. The women from Melanie's hen party had hit the dance floor, dragging her dad up there with them. She couldn't stop the grin forming on her face as she watched his special brand of dad dancing. At least she knew where she got her rhythm from.

Why wasn't she up there with them?

Why was she hiding by the bar, observing rather than joining in?

She'd made it through the day with what was left of her shattered heart aching, but she'd *made* it. She'd come through the other side and she was still standing. She hadn't fallen apart at the seams.

A record that had been hugely popular when she was a kid came on. Her grin widening, Hannah weaved through the tables to the dance floor and grabbed her father's hands. His answering smile was puzzled, shocked, even, but delighted all the same.

Their special brand of nonrhythmic dancing took off, a crowd quickly forming around them, the bride and groom hitting the floor, too.

She could do this. She could be a part of life. She didn't have to sit alone on the sidelines.

One of her sister's hen party tapped Hannah on the shoulder. 'Isn't that the man from Calvetti's?' she yelled above the music, pointing across the room.

Following the pointing finger, Hannah's heart jolted to see the tall figure she'd spotted leaning against the wall watching the dancing. Watching *her*.

She gave an absent nod in response, tuning out everything around her—everything except him.

Francesco.

Her stomach lurched heavily, feeling as if it had become detached from the rest of her.

He began to move, snaking his way round the packed tables, revellers parting on his approach in a manner that evoked the strongest sense of déjà vu.

Her heart flipped over to see him so groomed and utterly gorgeous in a snazzy pinstriped suit, the top buttons of his crisp blue shirt undone, exposing the top of his broad chest and the cross he wore around his neck....

Up close he looked in control and terrifying, the intent in his eyes showing he could eat her alive if she refused him anything.

Francesco crossed the dividing line onto the dance floor.

After the road trip from hell, he'd finally made it to her.

Nothing had come easy that day, the puncture on his tyre the last straw. By the time the helicopter had illegally landed to collect him, he'd been ready to rip someone's head off.

At last he stood before her. She'd frozen on the spot, her eyes big hazel pools of pain and bewilderment.

What had he done to her?

He had no idea what was being played by the DJ and nor did he care. When he placed his hands on Hannah's hips and pulled her to him, the sound tuned out and he moved her in a rhythm all their own.

She looked so vulnerable in her traditional bridesmaid dress. She trembled in it, rigid in his arms yet quivering.

He could feel eyes from all directions fixed on them.

'What are you doing here?' she asked, not looking at him.

'I want us to talk.'

'I don't want to be anywhere near you.'

'I know.' He breathed her scent in. 'But *I* need to be near *you*.'

She moved to escape his arms but he tightened his hold, continuing to move her around the floor. 'I'm not letting you go anywhere, not until you've given me the chance to speak.'

'I'm not speaking to you here,' she hissed into his ear, her warm breath sending completely inappropriate tingles racing over his skin. 'This is my sister's wedding. These guests here are my family and my sister's friends.'

'And I should have been with you today, getting to know them, instead of leaving you to face it on your own, but I'm the bastard who let his thirst for revenge cause pain to the one person in the world he loves.'

He stopped dancing and looked at her. The pain in her eyes had gone, only stark bewilderment remaining.

'*You*,' he emphasised. 'I love *you*. I should have trusted fate when it brought you to me.'

'I don't want to hear it.' Her voice was hoarse, her cheeks flushed.

Her resistance was nothing less than he deserved. He released his tight hold and stepped back, keeping his hands on her arms so she couldn't run.

'Remember when I gave you five minutes of *my* time?' he said, reminding her of that time a month ago when she'd first begged for five minutes. If he'd known then what those five minutes would lead to, he would have locked himself away in his office without a second thought. What an arrogant fool he had been. 'Now I am asking for five minutes of *your* time.'

Had it really only been a month ago that she'd propositioned him?

How could his entire world transform in such a small timeframe?

'Believe me, if I could have that time again I would do everything differently,' she said, wriggling out of his hold. 'Let's go sit in the garden. But only because I don't want to have a scene in front of my family.'

* * *

The breeze had picked up since Hannah had sat in the garden with her mother. Now the evening party was in full swing, the peace she'd found then had gone, music and laughter echoing through the windows.

She sat on the same bench. A bunch of kids had escaped the party and were having a game of football with an empty can.

Francesco sat next to her, keeping a respectable distance. All the same, she could feel his heat. How she wished she didn't respond to him so physically. Her emotional reactions to him were bad enough without her treacherous body getting in on the act, too.

'Go on, then, what did you want to talk about?' she said, making a silent vow to not say another word for the duration of the next five minutes. If he started spouting any more nonsense about loving her she would walk away.

If he loved her he would never have let her face this day on her own.

'I want to tell you about my father,' Francesco said, surprising her with his opening thread.

Despite her vow to remain mute, she whispered, 'Your father?'

He breathed heavily. 'I always knew what a bastard he was, but he was my father and I respected him. God help me but I loved him. All I ever wanted was his respect. I turned a blind eye to so many of his activities but turned the blindest eye to what was happening right under my own roof.'

His eyes held hers, the chocolate fudge hard, almost black.

'I always knew my father was a violent man. To me that was normal. It was our way of life. I knew he craved respect. Again, that was normal. What I did not know until after his death four years ago was that he was one of mainland Europe's biggest suppliers of drugs. That was a blow, enough to make me despise him, but not enough to destroy all my memories of the man. But what I learned just a year ago when I discovered my mother's diaries was that he beat her throughout their marriage, cheated on her, and fed her the drugs that eventually killed her.'

When he reached for her hand she didn't pull away, not even when he clasped it so tightly she feared for her blood supply.

'She was seventeen when they married, an innocent. He was twenty-three years older and a brute from the start.' He practically spat the words out. 'He forced himself on her on their wedding night. He beat her for the first time on their honeymoon. I wish I'd known, but my mother did everything in her power to protect me from seeing too much. As a child it was normal for my mother to be bruised. We would laugh at how clumsy she was, but it was all a lie.'

He shook his head and dragged his fingers through his hair. 'I spent three days reading her diaries. When I finished I was filled with so much hate for the man. And *guilt*—how could I have been so blind? The man I hero-worshipped was nothing but a drug-peddling wife beater. He *wanted* her hooked—it was a means to control her. I swear if he hadn't been dead I would have killed him myself using my bare hands.'

Hannah shivered. Oh, poor, poor Francesco. She'd known he hated his father, but this? This was worse than she could ever have imagined.

Suddenly he let go of her hand and palmed her cheeks. 'I have spent the past eleven months eradicating everything that man built. Everything. The parties stopped, the womanising stopped. All I wanted was vengeance for my mother and, even though my father was rotting in hell, I was determined to destroy what was his. I'd already closed his

drug dens, but I resolved to annihilate everything else—
the armouries, the so-called legitimate businesses that were
in fact a front for money laundering—every last brick of
property. The one thing I wanted above all else, though,
was the Mayfair casino.'

Here, his eyes seemed to drill into hers. 'Years ago, my
father tried to get that casino. It was the only failure of his
life. He tried everything to get his hands on that place,
but Godfrey Renfrew refused to sell it to such a notorious gangster. That failure was a large thorn in my father's
side. For me to purchase that same property would mean I
had succeeded where he had failed, proof that I was a better man than him.'

'So you've won,' she said softly. 'You've got your vengeance.'

'No.' He shook his head for emphasis. 'I walked into that
room with the Mastrangelos today and knew I had lost. I
had lost because I had lost *you*. How could I be a better
man than him when I had let the most important person in
my world down for the sake of vengeance?'

He brushed his lips against hers, the heat of his breath
filling her senses, expanding her shrivelled heart.

'After speaking with the Mastrangelos, I called Godfrey earlier and withdrew my offer for the casino,' he whispered. 'I don't want it anymore. It's tainted. All I want is
you. That's if you'll have me. I wouldn't blame you if you
didn't.' He sighed and nuzzled into her cheek. 'You asked
me once if you scared me. The truth is you did—you scared
me because you made me feel, and because I knew I wasn't
worthy of you. The only real relationship I have as a refer-
ence is my parents', and witnessing that was like living in
one of Dante's circles of hell. You deserve so much better.'

'Not all marriages and relationships are like that.'

'Intellectually, I know that. Emotionally, though, it's

taken me a lot longer to accept it. I wanted to protect you from me. I looked at you and saw the innocence my mother had before she married my father. I didn't want to taint you.'

'How could you do that? You are not your father, Francesco. You're a mixture of both your parents and the uniqueness that is *you*. You're just you. No one else.'

He almost crushed her in his embrace. 'I swear I'll never hurt you again. Never. *You* make me a better man. Even if we leave here and head our separate ways, I will still be a better man for having known you.'

Tears pricked her eyes. Her heart felt so full she now feared it could burst.

Head their separate ways? Was that really what she wanted?

'I know how important your work is to you and I would never want to get in the way of that. Medicine is your life, but what I want to know—*need* to know—is if you can fit me into your life, too. Forget what I said about you not fitting into my world—it's *your* world *I* need to fit into. Let me in, I beg of you. I'm not perfect, not by any stretch of the imagination, but I swear on my mother's memory that I will love and respect you for the rest of my life.'

Hannah's chin wobbled. But she kept it together, refusing to let the tears fall. All the same, her voice sounded broken to her own ears. 'I love that you're not perfect.'

He stilled and pulled away to look at her. His eyes glittered with questions.

'Neither of us is perfect but…' She took a deep breath, trying to keep a hold of her racing heart. If Francesco, her big, arrogant bear of a man, could put his heart and pride on the line… She cupped his warm cheek. 'I think you're perfect for me.'

She'd barely got the words out before his mouth came

crashing down on hers, a kiss of such passion and longing that this time the tears really did fall.

'Don't cry, *amore*. Don't cry.' Francesco wiped her tears away and pressed his lips to her forehead. He wrapped his arms around her and she nestled her cheek against his chest.

He gave a rueful chuckle. 'I can't believe I worried about *you* getting burned. I should have known from the start—deep down I think I did—that, of the two of us, I was the more likely to be.'

'Oh, no, but you were right,' she confessed. 'And I'm glad I was so blasé about your concerns because if I'd known how badly you *would* burn me I would have run a mile.'

She tilted her chin back up to look at him. She felt light, as if the weight that had been compressing her insides for what felt like for ever had been lifted. 'You've brought me back to life and let colour back into my world. You make me whole and I want to be in your life, too. Your past, everything you've been through has shaped you into the man you are today and that's the man I've fallen in love with.'

'You really love me?'

For the first time Hannah saw a hint of vulnerability in Francesco's cool, confident exterior.

'More than anything. I didn't think I needed anyone. You've shown me that I do. Not just you, but my family, too.' She kissed his neck then whispered into his ear, 'You've also weaned me off my addiction to my phone. I've only checked it three times today.'

He threaded his long fingers through her hair, a deep laugh escaping his throat that deepened when he snagged a couple of knots, 'If I could trust myself not to break every bone in his body, I would pay another visit to that bastard who knocked you off your bike and thank him.'

'For bringing us together?'

'The stars aligned for us that morning.'

'Shame about my broken collarbone and concussion.'

'Not forgetting your poor finger.'

She giggled. She hadn't thought of her finger in weeks. 'I'm surprised you let him walk away without any injury.'

'He took one look at me in his doorway and virtually wet himself. I didn't need to touch him. If the same thing were to happen to you now, I doubt I would be so restrained.'

'Yes, you would,' she chided, rubbing her nose into his linen shirt.

'And you know that how?'

'Because you would never hurt me, and to cause physical injury to another human, especially in my name, would be to hurt me.'

'You still believe that? After what I did to you last night, you still believe in me?'

'I believe it more than ever.' And she did. She, more than anyone, knew the hold the past had on the present. All that mattered was that they didn't allow the past to shape their futures. 'In any case, I bet he'll spend the rest of his life having nightmares that you'll turn up on his doorstep again.'

'Good. He deserves it.' He gave a humourless chuckle. 'We should invite him to our wedding.'

'Why, are we getting married?'

'Too right we are. I love you, Dr Chapman, and I will love you for the rest of my life.'

'I love you, too, Signor Calvetti.'

He kissed her again. 'Dottore Hannah Calvetti. It has a nice ring to it.'

'Hmm…' Her lips curved into a contented smile. Francesco was right. It had a wonderful ring to it.

EPILOGUE

HANNAH WALKED CAREFULLY up the steep steps to the front door of the villa, happily inhaling the scent emitted by the overabundance of ripe lemon trees.

Francesco opened the door before she got to the top.

'*Buonasera, Dottore Calvetti,*' he said.

'Good evening, Signor Calvetti,' she replied, before slipping into fluent Sicilian-Italian. 'How has Luciano been today?'

'An angel. Well, he's been an angel since I relieved the nanny. I think he might have given her an extra grey hair or two today. He's definitely worn himself out—he fell asleep fifteen minutes ago. But enough of the small talk—how did you do?'

She couldn't hide the beam that spread across her face. 'I got the job!'

Francesco's face spread into an identical grin. He drew her to him and kissed her, then rubbed his nose to hers. 'I knew you could do it, you clever lady. In fact, Tino is at this moment preparing your favourite meal to celebrate.'

'Mussels in white wine?'

He nodded with a definite hint of smugness. 'Followed by hot chocolate-fudge cake.'

'I love you!' Tino, their chef, made the best chocolate-fudge cake in the world.

He laughed and tapped her bottom. 'Go shower and get changed. I'll open a bottle of wine.'

This time it was she who kissed him, hard.

'Before I forget, Melanie messaged me earlier,' she said. 'They can definitely come for the weekend.'

'Great. Let me know the times and I'll get the jet over to England for them.'

With a spring in her step, Hannah climbed the stone staircase and headed down the uneven corridor to their bedroom. As she passed their eighteen-month-old son's nursery, she poked her head through the door to find him in deep sleep. He didn't stir when she lowered the side of the cot to press a gentle kiss to his cheek. 'Night, night, sleep tight,' she whispered before slipping back out.

She opened her bedroom door and there, on her dressing table, was the most enormous bunch of roses she had ever seen, huge even by Francesco's standards.

His faith in her never ceased to amaze her.

Luciano had come into their lives more quickly than either had anticipated. Within two months of their marriage she'd fallen pregnant, which hadn't been all that surprising considering the laissez-faire approach to contraception they'd adopted.

When it came time for Hannah to take maternity leave, they'd uprooted to Sicily. It had been agreed that when her maternity was up they would move back to London. Except…she'd fallen in love with Sicily, with the people and the language. Besides, it was easier for Francesco to run his empire from there, so she saw more of him during the week than she had in London, and they hated having to spend nights away from each other.

Full of determination, she'd set about learning the language. She'd employed a tutor and within weeks had refused to answer Francesco or any of his staff unless they spoke in their native tongue. She had been determined to master it. And they had all been determined to help her.

'I got the job, Beth,' she said, speaking aloud in English, just in case Beth hadn't bothered to learn Italian with her. Now that she couldn't visit her grave so regularly, she had taken to simply talking to her whenever the mood struck. Sometimes, in her dreams, her twin spoke back. 'I'm going to work at the hospital on the children's ward here in Palermo and train for my consultancy here, too.'

All the pieces had come together.

She could not be happier.

* * * * *

COMING NEXT MONTH FROM
HARLEQUIN *Presents*

Available August 19, 2014

#3265 TYCOON'S TEMPTATION
The Chatsfield
by Trish Morey

Franco Chatsfield must secure a partnership with Holly Purman's vineyard, the family business she's devoted her whole life to. She'll give Franco six weeks to prove himself, but working together sends their senses reeling—one taste just isn't enough!

#3266 THE HOUSEKEEPER'S AWAKENING
At His Service
by Sharon Kendrick

Injured playboy Luis Martinez is sick of nurses and demands his sweet, innocent housekeeper Carly Conner massage him back to health! Whisked away to the south of France, how long will she be able to deny tantalizing tension between them?

#3267 MORE PRECIOUS THAN A CROWN
by Carol Marinelli

Prince Zahid, heir to the Kingdom of Ishla, once walked away from the fire blazing in Trinity Foster's eyes. Now, after one earth-shattering night, it's revealed that Trinity needs Zahid's protection. She's strictly forbidden, but walking away again may prove impossible....

#3268 CAPTURED BY THE SHEIKH
Rivals to the Crown of Kadar
by Kate Hewitt

Sheikh Khalil's first step to reclaiming his crown is to kidnap his rival's bride-to-be, Elena Karras. Expecting a cold, convenient marriage, this virgin queen is instead carried into the sands, where she discovers an unexpected desire for her sinfully sexy captor!

HPCNM0814RA

#3269 A NIGHT IN THE PRINCE'S BED
by Chantelle Shaw
For deaf theater actress Mina Hart, one night with a gorgeous stranger turns into headline news when he's revealed as Prince Aksel of Storvhal. Trapped in icy Scandinavia, can Mina rely on her senses to read this intensely private prince?

#3270 DAMASO CLAIMS HIS HEIR
One Night With Consequences
by Annie West
The virtue behind Princess Marisa's scandalous reputation touched a place in Damaso Pires that he'd thought long destroyed. But their brief affair becomes permanent when Marisa reveals she's pregnant.... There's only one way for Damaso to claim his heir—marriage!

#3271 CHANGING CONSTANTINOU'S GAME
by Jennifer Hayward
All bets are off when reporter Isabel Peters is dropped into Alexios Constantinou's lap during a hellish elevator ride—especially when he discovers that her next story is *him!* With everything at stake, he'll need a whole new game plan....

#3272 THE ULTIMATE REVENGE
The 21st Century Gentleman's Club
by Victoria Parker
Nicandro Santos is determined to bring down the ultra-prestigious *Q Virtus* gentleman's club. But with his enemy's daughter, Olympia Merisi, now in charge, the battle lines between this pair soon blur, and they risk entering more *sensual* territory....

YOU CAN FIND MORE INFORMATION ON UPCOMING HARLEQUIN® TITLES, FREE EXCERPTS AND MORE AT WWW.HARLEQUIN.COM.

HPCNM0814RB

REQUEST YOUR FREE BOOKS!

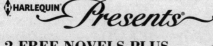 HARLEQUIN *Presents*

2 FREE NOVELS PLUS
2 FREE GIFTS!

YES! Please send me 2 FREE Harlequin Presents® novels and my 2 FREE gifts (gifts are worth about $10). After receiving them, if I don't wish to receive any more books, I can return the shipping statement marked "cancel." If I don't cancel, I will receive 6 brand-new novels every month and be billed just $4.30 per book in the U.S. or $4.99 per book in Canada. That's a saving of at least 14% off the cover price! It's quite a bargain! Shipping and handling is just 50¢ per book in the U.S. and 75¢ per book in Canada.* I understand that accepting the 2 free books and gifts places me under no obligation to buy anything. I can always return a shipment and cancel at any time. Even if I never buy another book, the two free books and gifts are mine to keep forever.

106/306 HDN FVRK

Name _____ (PLEASE PRINT) _____

Address _____ Apt. # _____

City _____ State/Prov. _____ Zip/Postal Code _____

Signature (if under 18, a parent or guardian must sign) _____

Mail to the Harlequin® Reader Service:
IN U.S.A.: P.O. Box 1867, Buffalo, NY 14240-1867
IN CANADA: P.O. Box 609, Fort Erie, Ontario L2A 5X3

**Are you a current subscriber to Harlequin Presents books
and want to receive the larger-print edition?
Call 1-800-873-8635 or visit www.ReaderService.com.**

* Terms and prices subject to change without notice. Prices do not include applicable taxes. Sales tax applicable in N.Y. Canadian residents will be charged applicable taxes. Offer not valid in Quebec. This offer is limited to one order per household. Not valid for current subscribers to Harlequin Presents books. All orders subject to credit approval. Credit or debit balances in a customer's account(s) may be offset by any other outstanding balance owed by or to the customer. Please allow 4 to 6 weeks for delivery. Offer available while quantities last.

Your Privacy—The Harlequin® Reader Service is committed to protecting your privacy. Our Privacy Policy is available online at www.ReaderService.com or upon request from the Harlequin Reader Service.

We make a portion of our mailing list available to reputable third parties that offer products we believe may interest you. If you prefer that we not exchange your name with third parties, or if you wish to clarify or modify your communication preferences, please visit us at www.ReaderService.com/consumerchoice or write to us at Harlequin Reader Service Preference Service, P.O. Box 9062, Buffalo, NY 14269. Include your complete name and address.

HP13

SPECIAL EXCERPT FROM

HARLEQUIN®

Presents®

Kate Hewitt brings you the first book in her new duet,
RIVALS TO THE CROWN OF KADAR—*tales of steamy
passion and seduction set among the desert sands.
Read on for an exclusive extract from*
CAPTURED BY THE SHEIKH:

* * *

SHE wanted him to kiss her.

His head dipped and her heart seemed to stop and then soar. His lips were so close now that if she moved at all they would be touching his. They would be kissing.

Yet she didn't move, transfixed as she was by both wonder and fear, and Khalil didn't move, either.

The moment stretched between them, suspended, endless.

His breath came out in a shudder and his hands tightened around her face. She tried to say something but words eluded her; all she could do was feel. Want.

Then with another shuddering breath he closed that small space between their mouths and his lips touched hers in her first and most wonderful kiss.

She let out a tiny sigh both of satisfaction and surrender, her hands coming up to tangle in the surprising softness of his hair. Her lips parted and Khalil deepened the kiss, pulling her closer as his tongue delved into her mouth, and everything in Elena throbbed powerfully to life.

She'd never known she could feel like this, want like this. It was so intense and sweet it almost felt painful. She pressed against him, acting on an instinct she hadn't realised she possessed. Khalil slid his hand from her face to cup her breast, and a shocked gasp escaped her mouth as exquisite sensation darted through her.

Khalil withdrew, dropping his hand and easing back from her so she felt a rush of loss. He reached up to cover her hands with his own and draw them down to her own lap.

"I shouldn't have…" he began, then shook his head. Even in the moonlit darkness she could see the regret and remorse etched on his harsh features.

"I wanted you to," she blurted, and he just shook his head again.

"You should sleep again, if you can," he said quietly, and Elena bit her lip, blinking hard. She wondered, with a rush of humiliation, if she'd actually been the one to kiss him. In that moment it had been hard to tell, and she'd wanted it so much….

* * *

Don't miss
CAPTURED BY THE SHEIKH by Kate Hewitt
September 2014

Sharon Kendrick brings you her sensational story of temptation, seduction and so much more!

Sick of nurses fussing over him, injured playboy Luis Martinez demands that his innocent housekeeper massage him back to health.

Carly Conner has spent her life trying not to be noticed. But now that her boss is looking at her differently, how long can she deny the tantalizing tension between them…?

THE HOUSEKEEPER'S AWAKENING
by
Sharon Kendrick

Available September 2014,
wherever books and ebooks are sold.